Destiny's Wish

Cedar Grove Medical: Book Two

Marissa Dobson

Published by Sunshine Press
Printed in the United States of America
ISBN-13: 978-1-939978-59-2

$\mathcal{D}$edication

To my husband who has supported me through thick and thin.

To my readers who loved Hope's Toy Chest and wanted more from Cedar Grove Medical. Thank you for your help with the research necessary for this book. For sharing your stories of hope, courage, and devastation.

To everyone who pushed for this book. My wonderful editor, Rosa, my beta readers, and proofers you're an amazing team. To Allyson, my talented assistant, who helps me set up wonderful online events.

Destiny's Wish: Cedar Grove Medical

Contents

Destiny's Wish: Cedar Grove Medical

After Nora Horton's husband dies while serving his country, she is left alone to raise their beautiful daughter, Destiny. She picks up the pieces and moves on, but when Destiny's cancer returns, Nora isn't sure she can handle it any longer. She's not certain she can be strong for her daughter while she's falling apart inside.

Doctor Brian West is a pediatric cardiologist at Cedar Grove Children's Hospital and has seen many sick children during his years there. He has always been able to do his job without letting it get to him, because he knows if he's distracted for even a minute, someone might die and it would be on him. When he stumbles upon Nora, the recognition is instant and he can't distance himself from her or her sick little girl, especially not when the child tells him her wish.

Destiny's dying wish isn't meant for her mother's ears…because what she wants more than anything is for her mother to have someone to love.

Destiny's Wish: Cedar Grove Medical

Chapter One

In the hallway, Nora Horton gazed into one of the hospital's playrooms where children frolicked. She sat clutching the documents that confirmed her biggest fear; her daughter's cancer was back and this time worse than before. With the dreadful news upon her, the pink and red hearts, cheery Valentine's Day decorations, seemed out of place. Her whole world crashed around her and the bright colors made her want to scream and rip them into tiny pieces. It seemed wrong that things should appear so beautiful when in reality it was quite the opposite.

There in the middle of the room, her daughter, Destiny, and another little girl with a scarf around her head played with dolls. If it wasn't for the pajamas, headscarves, and the unmistakable stench of the hospital, she could almost picture the girls playing anywhere other than the cancer ward of Cedar Grove Children's Hospital. She stood to get a better view of the smiles etched on their faces. *Enjoy these moments, because soon she'll be too tired to get out of bed.*

The very scene before her made her want to take Destiny and run as far and as fast as they could. But no one could outrun cancer, no matter how hard they tried. Instead, they had to fight against it. If her daughter was going to stand a chance against the cancer, they'd have to fight doubly hard with chemotherapy and radiation at the same time. Even then, the chances of remission were slim.

Their last battle against cancer had been rough. There had been times she wasn't sure they'd make it through, but her gut told her it was going to be nothing like what the future had in store for them. Her baby girl needed her to be strong, but it seemed like everything was falling apart around her. This helplessness and sorrow that spread through her like poison was worse than when the Army officers showed up at her door to tell her that her husband had been killed while serving overseas. First her husband was stolen from her, and now her daughter might be as well. Neither of them even had a chance to truly live.

"Oh, Jim, I wish you were here." She took a deep breath and tried to push away the tears that were threatening to fall. No matter how hard she tried to hold things together, her world was crashing down around her. Black dots danced in her vision and her legs threatened to give out from under her. She swayed on her feet, then shot a hand out to grab hold of something to steady herself. The only thing available was the wall, so she pressed her hand against it.

"Ma'am…Ma'am, are you okay?"

She wasn't sure who had spoken to her, but even if she wanted to turn to look she couldn't have. Her body was fighting against yet another dose of devastation.

Someone touched her shoulder and her legs gave out from under her.

"Whoa there, I've got you." He wrapped his arms around her and helped lower her to the bench.

"I'm fine." She wasn't sure if she was trying to convince herself or the kind stranger who had come to her rescue.

"I don't think you are. Why don't you come with me and we'll get you checked out?"

For the first time, she tipped her head to look at him and realized the stranger who had come to her aid wasn't another parent, or a nurse. The man now sitting beside her was clad in a white lab coat. He was a doctor. She wasn't sure of his specialty but she had seen him around the hospital often.

"Are you okay?" someone else intoned.

Nora turned to find the nurse with long curly brown hair who had been so sweet to Destiny, but at that moment she couldn't remember the woman's name. Cheryl? Cara? No, it was Carly.

"Destiny," Nora mumbled.

"She's fine. She's playing. Why don't you take a break? Get something to eat. I'll be here with her."

"That sounds like a good idea," the doctor said as the nurse headed back into the playroom. "Let's see if you're okay."

"I'm fine. I just haven't eaten." She ran her hand over her forehead, trying to ease the pounding in her head. "I'll get something after I get Destiny back to her room."

"I have to insist you have something now." He tipped his head toward the small family waiting room at the end of the hall. "You're going to be in no condition to help her if you're sick."

"Help her…" Tears swam in her eyes again. "No one can help my baby girl. She's got cancer."

"Then it's even more important that you get something to eat. She'll need you strong for the fight she has ahead." He stopped an older nurse who was walking down the hall. "Nancy, would you mind popping downstairs and grabbing two sandwiches from the café, while I help this lady to the family room at the end of the hall? Tell them to put it on my account and I'll be down later. Get yourself something as well."

"Sure, Doctor West." She turned on her heels and headed back toward the elevators.

"You shouldn't have done that."

He glanced back at her. "Don't get me wrong, if it hadn't been Nancy I'd have gotten the sandwiches myself. Nancy and I go way back. She's a doll and I know she wouldn't think I was taking advantage of her. Now, are you okay to stand? I'd like to get you somewhere more comfortable."

She nodded and he helped her stand, keeping an arm around her as they made their way to the family room. "By the way, I'm Nora Horton. I've gathered you're *Doctor Somebody*, but do you have a name?"

"Nora Horton…it can't be." He glanced at her and smiled. "I don't believe it."

"Yeah, I'm positive I'm Nora Horton. Do I know you?"

"Brian West. It's been years since we've seen each other. How's Jim?" He closed the door to the family room, giving them privacy.

"He's…" She took hold of the back of the chair. Everything flooded back; images of Brian and Jim spending time together filled her thoughts. "Jim was killed in action more than six years ago. I was pregnant with Destiny…he didn't even know he was going to be a father."

"Oh, Nora." He squeezed her against him, hugging her gently. "I'm so sorry. I didn't know."

"How could you? You were halfway across the country, in the middle of your last year as a medical student, and it had been months since we'd spoken. I'm sorry I never called. I was a mess." She looked at him again, but this time she actually recognized him. It wasn't that he'd changed that much over the years, it was more that she had blocked him out of her memories.

Brian and Jim had been best friends. Both military brats, so they had bonded quickly. Even when Jim chose the Marines and Brian headed off to college, then medical school, they were still close. It had just been the last few months before his death that they'd lost contact. She was sure they'd have reconnected if he hadn't been killed; now they would never know.

"We hadn't lived there long but the women from the base gathered around and made sure I got through it. Otherwise, I don't know what I'd have done. I didn't believe it at first, then the anger that he'd been taken before he knew I was pregnant sank in." She twirled the necklace with their wedding bands that she always wore. "My whole pregnancy, I was a mess, but when Destiny came along…"

"Let's sit down, you still look too pale." He took hold of her arm again and guided her toward one of the small sofas.

"When…" She took a deep breath and continued. "When Destiny was born, I had to put my life back together. I never forgot Jim, but I had to move past my grief for her sake. That's how she got her name, it was my destiny to reclaim a life for her. Now this…"

"Who's her oncologist?" He took her hand.

"I don't know." She shook her head. "Jacobson or someone."

A knock at the door echoed through the room. "Come in," he hollered without turning away from her.

"Your sandwiches and fresh coffee from downstairs. None of that crappy stuff." She laid the sandwiches on the coffee table in front of them. "Nora, Carly told me you were ill before, are you feeling better now?"

She forced herself to smile at the kind nurse. "I was a little lightheaded, that's all. Stress and not eating, I guess it all plays a part."

"That it does." Nancy nodded. "You enjoy your lunch and Carly will take good care of Destiny. Don't worry about a thing."

"Thank you, Nancy. Nora and I are old friends, I'll see to her for a bit." He waited until the nurse left before turning back to Nora. "Let's eat and then I have a doctor I want you to meet with."

"No offense, but I've seen enough doctors for one day, Hell, for a lifetime." She took the plastic container he handed her and opened it. Inside was a turkey and swiss sandwich, with pasta salad off to the side.

"If you'll take my advice, you'll want him. Doctor Mathews is the Chief of Pediatric Oncology. He's the best one to handle Destiny's care, and I don't just say that because we're somewhat related through marriage." He laid his free hand on her leg, his gaze drilling into her. "Let me help you and Destiny."

"Somewhat related?"

"I see you didn't flat out tell me no, so I'll take that as a step in the right direction." He smirked and took a bite of his sandwich. "I'm not sure you met my brother, Jason. He's a pediatric surgeon here. Well, his wife Liz is Doctor Mathews's sister. See, somewhat family. More importantly, he can help."

"Why do you want to help us? It's been years and you don't even know Destiny." She took a small bite of the sandwich and her empty stomach nearly revolted.

"It has been years, but I'd like to think that at one time we were close friends. It wasn't just Jim and I, the three of us were close. Do you disagree?"

"Time changes people."

He shook his head as he chewed. "Not that much. Just because we haven't spoken in a while, doesn't mean you shouldn't let me help. Destiny needs whatever help she can get. Let's meet with Kingsley.

While oncology isn't my specialty, sign the form allowing me access to her chart so I can understand her needs. We'll get her through this."

"Doctor Jacobson suggested a chemotherapy and radiation combination. He said it was her only chance. The last time she did radiation treatments alone, they were rough. I don't know how she'll handle both at the same time."

"Jacobson is a good doctor, but there might be other options. Kingsley would know. He keeps up to date with all the newest treatment options, and I know there's another child in the hospital who's in an experimental trial. That might be possible for Destiny." He polished off the rest of his sandwich and leaned back. "Half a sandwich isn't much, but I don't suspect you're going to finish the rest. How about we take a stroll and see if we can find Kingsley?"

Part of her wanted to tell him she could do it herself just to prove she was strong enough to get through this again, that she wasn't without a backbone and wouldn't crumble to the ground. But this wasn't about her, it was about Destiny. Her daughter needed the best doctors she could get. Putting her pride aside, she took a deep breath and accepted his offer of assistance for Destiny's sake.

Chapter Two

The next morning, Brian sat behind the desk in his office, still questioning why he had gotten involved. His sister-in-law would say he had a soft spot for women who needed help. If that was the case, this was one woman he should have run away from. Not only was she trying to deal with her daughter's cancer, but she was still grieving for her husband. The one thing she didn't need was him trying to make amends to her dead husband's memory.

He'd meant to read over Destiny's file last night, but an emergency had called him back to the hospital before he got a chance. Now there were patients that needed his care, but he wanted to pull the file out and see exactly what the little girl was up against. It might have been against his better judgment, but he was going to stay involved to make sure everything that could be done for her was being done. He'd let Jim down once; he'd be damned if he'd let him down again.

"Doctor West, do you have a moment?"

He glanced up to find Nancy standing in the doorway. It was somewhat surprising since she wasn't a nurse on his floor. While they had known each other for years, their usual socializing happened outside of the hospital. "Sure, come in." He nodded to the chair across from his desk.

"I wanted to speak with you about Mrs. Norton." She took a seat in front of him. "She's extremely fragile right now and—"

"Nancy, if you are implying I'm trying to take advantage of a situation…"

"No, absolutely not. Actually, I came here to convince you to help her. You said you're an old friend, then be there for her. She has no one, no family, and no friends here. She's living out of a motel when she leaves the hospital."

"A motel?" He was appalled. "Kingsley won't discharge Destiny unless she has somewhere safe and clean to go to."

"Her house is on the market and she left everything behind to bring Destiny here. She claims she's looking for a place so she can have somewhere nearby for when the child is released, but she rarely leaves the hospital. Talk to her, explain what she needs to do." Nancy leaned forward. "I don't know what I expect you to do. We've all tried, but she just says she wants to be with her daughter. As you've seen today, she's not eating. I don't know when she actually slept more than a few winks in that chair next to Destiny."

"I'll talk to her." Ideas rushed through his mind as he considered how he might help her.

"Just one last thing." She smirked at him. "Doctor Jacobson isn't very happy you've gone over his head and gotten Doctor Mathews to take over Destiny's care. He's been very vocal that he doesn't appreciate you pulling family strings to get specialized care for her."

"He knows where to find me if he wishes to voice his disagreement. I won't apologize for helping a friend, or for allowing Nora to explore all the options open to her."

Nancy stood but didn't move away from the desk. "It might be none of my business but I have to ask. How well do you know her?"

"Well enough that I'd go to bat for her." He leaned forward, placing his hands on his desk. "Her late husband and I were best friends. He's not here to look after them, to make sure Destiny gets the best care she can, but I am. I'll do right by him and his family." *Unlike the last time.* The guilt turned his stomach until his chest tightened with regret.

"Brian, we need to talk." Kingsley stood in the doorway.

"Seems like I've installed a rotating door to my office." He shook his head. "Come in."

"I was just leaving." Nancy rose, then turned back to Brian. "Thank you. I hope you can help her."

With Nancy gone, he turned his attention to Kingsley. "What can I do for you?"

"Have you looked over the Horton file?" He took the chair Nancy had vacated, stretching his long legs out in front of him.

"Not yet. I had a few things to attend to once I left Nora with you, and just when I was about to, Nancy stopped by. Why?"

"Her cancer is aggressive, but I think she could be a candidate for the study that's about to start. I've spoken to Mrs. Norton about it, but she has some reservations. I've sent you all the information on the study. Look over it and please talk to her. The trial begins on Monday and she'll need to go through the pre-testing."

"Does it give her a better success rate than the treatment Jacobson was suggesting?"

Kingsley brought his ankle up to rest on his other knee. "For Destiny's condition I believe it does, but more importantly it isn't radiation. Reading over her chart, you'll see what a hard time the child had the first time they did radiation. I believe she's had one of the worst cases of radiation sickness I've seen, but the worst part was the radiation burns she suffered. She was two when she went through it the first time, which made things harder for Nora."

"I'm done for the day, so I'll read over everything and then go down and talk to her." He rubbed the bridge of his nose and tried not to think of the turmoil Nora was going through. "I was heading down there in a bit anyway. That's why Nancy was here, she wants me to convince Nora she needs to find an apartment."

"Good, because I can't sign off on a release until she's living somewhere suitable. This experiment might not be as bad as radiation, but Destiny's immune system will still be compromised more than it is already. A motel is no place for a sick child."

"I think Nora understands that, but she's wanted to be close to the hospital. I think if she knew her daughter might be released, she'd be more willing to find something. She wants to get her daughter home and healthy." Brian hoped he wasn't going out on a limb by saying that.

"She was admitted because of her breathing, but that has improved. If she has suitable living conditions, the child could be discharged. It should be somewhere close if possible, since she'll have to be here almost daily for treatments. Unless her condition deteriorates, there's no need for her to be hospitalized."

"I'll see to it that she has a place by the end of the week." He swallowed, knowing he might have just bitten off more than he could chew. It had been years since he had to find an apartment, so he had no idea how difficult it might be.

"Well, if you convince her to do the study we can have the tests done tomorrow and she'll have a few days with her daughter before things begin. I'm sure Destiny could use some time with her mom, without being in the hospital. They can try to forget about this place for a few days." Kingsley rose from the chair. "You've got my number if she has any more questions about the study that you can't answer."

"If she decides not to do it, what course of treatment are you recommending?" Brian asked before Kingsley could leave.

"The same thing Jacobson recommended. Radiation is the best treatment, and the chemotherapy on top of it should hopefully ensure the cancer cells do not return. So for Destiny's sake it would be best to do the study. I can't make any guarantees on how she will handle the treatment but from the cases I've seen so far, I believe it would be better for her. Convince her, it's in the girl's best interest." With that,

Kingsley strolled from the office, leaving Brian alone with his thoughts.

He wasn't sure how he was going to convince Nora that the experimental treatment was the best option, but in order to do that he needed to familiarize himself with her condition, and the treatments. Then he'd go to her with the facts. She wanted what was best for Destiny and so did he. He didn't even want to think about the fact she still needed a place to live. One problem at a time.

Whatever he had to do, he'd do because they needed him.

Chapter Three

Nora pulled her legs up onto the chair and stared down at her sleeping daughter. She had no idea what she was going to do about this experimental treatment option. Was it worth it, considering it was questionable? Or would they be back to doing the chemotherapy and radiation combination in a few months? Would the cancer be worse then? All the questions circled her thoughts, but no answers emerged from the fog.

"Oh, Jim, I wish you were here with us." She wrapped her hand around the necklace, his ring warm from the touch of her skin, and she was unable to hold back the tears. She hugged her legs and wept. One good cry and then she'd shove the pieces of herself back into something presentable, even if that meant she'd have to use tape to hold it together.

"Nora." A voice whispered from behind her.

She turned to find Brian standing in the doorway, his white lab coat gone. With the back of her hand, she wiped away the tears. "Come in. I figured you'd have gone home hours ago."

"I was in my office going over her file. Why don't we grab some coffee and talk? That way we won't disturb her."

She glanced at her daughter. "I shouldn't leave her."

"We'll just be down the hall in the staff lounge and you can see her room from there. We'll get some coffee and talk." When she still didn't move, he stepped closer. "I want to talk to you about the treatment options."

"I've already heard all about them from Doctor Mathews and Jacobson."

"You might have, and maybe I'm wrong, but I think you'd like to know what I would recommend. If I'm wrong, stay here with Destiny, but if you want to know what I'd recommend I'll be in the lounge. End of the hall, the door will be open." Without another word, he turned on his heels and left.

She sat there for a moment, stunned. She wanted to know what he thought was best because right now she was so torn, but the way he'd brushed her off stung. Instead of just sitting there, she stood, pulling the blanket up around her daughter. When Destiny didn't stir, she stepped closer to the door and with one last deep breath she left the room. She'd find out what he thought and then get back to her daughter before she even woke up.

Many of the rooms were already dark. Some parents camped out by the bedsides of their children, while other kids were alone. She couldn't help but feel sorry for the children who were by themselves, surrounded by all the scary aspects of medical technology. At least the nurses on this floor were some of the best she had met. They were kind, caring, and always there to help soothe a child.

"I see you decided to join me." Brian stood in the doorway, two mugs of coffee in his hands.

"Do you have a thing about doorways?" He raised an eyebrow at her and she smirked. "Seems like this is the third time I've seen you hovering in a doorway in the last several hours."

"To be around you, I'd hover in every doorway." He held out a mug to her.

Her heart skipped a beat at his statement. She wasn't sure if it was loneliness that make her think he was flirting with her, or if he really was. Either way it was like a direct line to send her heart fluttering. She swallowed and forced her heartbeat to calm. She was a mother with a very sick child; there was no time for flirting or anything else in her future. Destiny had to be her only priority.

"Come sit down." He motioned to the table just inside. It had a clear view back to Destiny's room. "Since you're here, I'm assuming you want to know what I'd recommend."

"Or maybe I came to tell you to leave us alone." She clung to the mug, soaking up the warmth.

"You were always feisty but I don't think you'd do that. Not now."

"Why, because I'm alone?" She set down the mug and leaned closer. "I've been alone most of my life and it's never stopped me before. Plus, I'm not alone, I've got Destiny and she's all that really matters."

"If you'd have given me a chance to answer, I would have said no. I think you want to know what I'd recommend because you're scared you're going to make the wrong decision." He held up a hand before she could interrupt. "There's no reason to deny it. Every parent feels just what you're going through right now. They're overwhelmed, terrified, and trying to keep it together for the sake of their child."

She took a sip of the coffee before she finally nodded. "Then what do you think I should do?"

"I've spent the last few hours gathering all the facts so I could come here and give you what I know. Now that I'm sitting here, I don't think that's enough. I think you need more than that. So, I'll tell you that I think it's Destiny's best option and that if it was my daughter in that bed I'd do it."

"You'd do it even though the risks aren't completely known? They can't be sure it will be beneficial."

"That's the one thing about medicine, you never know completely. What works for one patient might not work for the next. Don't think that just because I'm a doctor and actually understand the mumbo-jumbo that's in the documents that I have all the answers." He reached across the table and laid his hand over hers. "It's a way to avoid the radiation that she had such a hard time with last time. One that has a good chance of helping her."

"A good chance! Why can't anyone give me a guarantee that this will cure her?" She took deep breaths, trying to calm herself. "This isn't fair, she hasn't even began to live her life and now she's got to fight to live again. Last time was hard enough but now it seems like it's back with a vengeance. What did we do to deserve this?"

"It's not something you've done. Cancer is an awful thing, but it's not a punishment for a wrong you've committed in the past. I don't know why it picks some and not others, or why it comes back when others get to stay in remission the rest of their lives."

They spent the next twenty minutes going over all of the questions she had, but in the end he still couldn't give her the guarantee she wanted. It was a risk, one that she had to take. She'd have to sign off on the documents allowing it. It was her decision and no one else could make it. If things went disastrous, it would be her fault in the end. She just had to hope this experimental treatment was better than what they went through with the radiation.

She bit the bullet and nodded. "Okay, I'll sign the papers."

"Good." He stood and refilled their coffee mugs. "Now for the other thing I wanted to discuss with you."

"If it's another decision about her care, I'm not sure I can handle it tonight." She brought her hand to her mouth as she tried to stifle a yawn.

"Actually, it's about your living arrangements."

"I keep telling everyone things are fine."

He took his seat across from her and shook his head. "Things aren't fine, you're living in a motel."

"It's what I've found and it's close. I don't need an apartment when I'm always here."

"I know Nancy explained to you that you need something if you want Destiny to be discharged. Have you been looking?"

She leaned back against the hard chair and let out a light laugh. "With what free time? I'm by her bedside night and day. There's no one else. I don't have time to go out and look for an apartment, especially when it's not like they will discharge her anytime soon."

"I have it on good authority that she could be discharged as early as tomorrow afternoon if you had somewhere to go. It would give you a few days with her without being surrounded by all the medical reminders of what lies ahead."

She scooted her chair back and stood. "Why tell me this now? It's too late to find somewhere tonight. You said she will have tests done tomorrow which means I can't leave either. Why give me hope only to have it dashed?"

"I can't believe you haven't been looking for something. You had to realize she'd be discharged at some point."

She took hold of the back of the chair, not sure if she was angrier at him for dropping this on her now or at herself for not considering the future. "It was so bad last time that she was in the hospital almost her entire treatment. I guess I figured it would be the same this time. Why find an apartment when she wouldn't get to come home with me? It wouldn't be a home without her. The motel was just a place to keep our stuff, because her hospital room has felt more like home than the room there."

They sat for a moment, silence thick around them. "What am I going to do? It's not like apartments are easy to find in this area, especially not close to the hospital."

"Come home with me."

She tipped her heard toward him, unable to believe what she'd just heard. "Excuse me?"

"I've got a house a few miles outside of the city and there's plenty of room for the two of you. It will give you a place to stay while you're looking for an apartment. That way Destiny can be discharged and you can spend some time with her until the treatments begin. Do something fun and try to forget what Monday brings."

"I can't…"

He shook his head. "Don't say you can't. You don't want to, maybe, but it isn't that you can't."

"I was going to say I couldn't impose on you."

He polished off the last of his coffee and stood to put the mug in the dishwasher. "It's the least I can do, we're friends. This way after the tests are done tomorrow, she can be discharged. Otherwise she might not get to feel the cool air on her face while she can still enjoy it. You said it yourself earlier…since the treatments haven't begun yet, she's doing okay. Neither of us know what she'll feel like once they begin, so why not get her out of here for a bit? Let her be a kid, even if it's only for a short period."

"This is your home we're talking about. You don't just invite people to move in." She ran a head over her face. As much as she wanted to accept the offer so she could get a good night's sleep in a bed, and take a hot bath, she felt guilty.

"Why? It's not like you're a stranger." He leaned against the small kitchenette counter. "The house is plenty big enough that you don't have to see me if you don't want to. Plus, I'm here more than I'm home. You'll only have to worry about Greta."

"Your wife?" She glanced down at his hand, but didn't see a ring.

"No." He let out a light laugh that caressed across her skin. "She's the housekeeper. She kind of came with the house, and trust me she'd love to have others around. Someone to take care of."

"I thought that type of thing had been done away with long ago."

"I purchased the house from another doctor here at the hospital. It was a house I knew I wanted when I first walked in. I was there for a Christmas party and I told him if he ever wanted to sell it, to let me know. I guess it was about two years later, he was retiring, and moving to Hawaii with his wife. It's where his son was stationed with the Navy and they just loved it there. Anyway, I bought the house on the condition I'd keep Greta on. She had been raised in the house. Her mother was the housekeeper there, and then Greta took over. It seemed wrong to push her out the house, so I agreed. Just being me, I don't have much use for a housekeeper, but it works out nicely for both of us."

"She can't be happy not having much to do. I mean, if you're never there, how much can you mess it up? With your long hours, there'd be limited cooking for you." She realized she was rambling. "Guess I never pictured you with household staff."

"Not staff, just Greta, and I don't consider her staff. She's family, at least she's become family. So, what do you say, will you come stay with us?"

The way he leaned against the counter, smirking at her so full of confidence, made her want to go to him. The way his dark hair fell just above his eyes made her wanted to push it away. It had been so long since she had any urges like this. She wasn't sure how to handle them. *Focus.* She tried to listen to her own advice, but it was like the woman in her was coming alive again after all these years and was demanding to be set free.

Destiny's Wish: Cedar Grove Medical

Chapter Four

The minutes ticked by as Brian waited for Nora's answer with his heart in his throat. Insanity could be the only explanation for his offer. Sure, Jim and Nora had opened up their place to him whenever he was traveling through, but inviting her and Destiny to live with him was different. This wasn't just for a visit with an end date in sight, this was an open invitation to his home. The one place he might not spend much time at but had always been his sanctuary from the stresses of his work.

Even knowing his privacy was going to be disturbed didn't worry him. If he was honest with himself, he might even admit he could use the change, the distraction, and the company. He had been alone for so long, the idea of having someone around was exciting and a little nerve-racking.

"Destiny could really be discharged tomorrow?"

He nodded. "The pre-testing would be done in the morning and then she could go…as long as you have a place to stay. You don't have many options. It's either my place or you try to find somewhere tomorrow, but then you'd have to deal with the utilities and move in."

"You have the room." She tucked a strand of her hair behind her ear. "I mean…it would only be for a couple of days while I find a place. With Destiny out of here, I can take her with me when we look around."

"I wouldn't have offered if I didn't have the room. The house has six bedrooms, so there's plenty of rooms for you and Destiny to choose from."

"Six." Her voice was hitched up a notched in shock.

"I was young and stupid when I bought the house." He smirked. "I thought one day I'd have a family of my own to make the house a true home and all the rooms would be filled. That and I wanted the entertaining space. I still host a Christmas party there every year."

"Jim always said you would settle down and have a dozen kids. That you'd have the all-American family everyone envied." The smile she gave him didn't quite meet her eyes.

"I'm really sorry about Jim." He was sorrier than she knew, for the last conversation with Jim was one he'd never be able to shake. There was no re-do, or even a chance to make up for the statements that had been said now that Jim was dead. "What do you say, will you take me up on my offer?"

She took a deep breath and nodded. "I feel like I'm imposing, but there's very little I wouldn't do to get Destiny out of here. If you're sure you don't mind, then yes. We'll start looking and hopefully will find somewhere by the week's end."

"Honest, there's no rush. You should focus on your daughter, do something that will help you both forget what Monday brings. There's nothing you can do yet and worrying about what the treatments are going to be like will only make you sick." He stepped away from the counter and walked toward her. "Actually, I'm off on Friday, so how about we make use of the pool and then I'll throw something on the grill?"

"Destiny loves to swim but I'm not sure that's such a good idea. It's February, two weeks before Valentine's Day. It's freezing. How could we possibly do that?"

"It's an indoor pool. Heated, and she won't even have to go outside." He laid his hand over hers. "I'm a doctor, after all. I wouldn't recommend anyone swimming outdoors at this time of year."

She let out a light chuckle and her shoulder brushed against his. "I didn't think it was outdoors. I figured you were referring to a public indoor pool and I didn't think it was a good idea for her to have to be outside after swimming, even if it was just to the car." She paused, her whole body going still. "Wait, you have an indoor pool? This house of yours must be a mansion."

"Not a mansion, but let's say it has all the comforts one could want." His house was one thing he was proud of. It was a gem hidden just outside the city, with enough land to give him a peaceful surrounding, yet still close enough to the hospital and downtown. When he sat outside, there wasn't any city noise. Just birds chirping, and occasionally he'd catch deer grazing where the lawn merged into the trees on the back half of his property. Peace, that's what he had there.

"Well, I'm looking forward to seeing it."

"If you want to give me the key to your room, I can retrieve your belongings and have them at the house waiting for you."

"There's no need. There's not much and I'll have to go to the motel and check out anyway." She tipped her head toward him. "I sold or donated most of our belongings. We only brought what would fit into the car, so once I find a place if it's not furnished, I'll have to purchase all the household supplies and furniture again. It just seemed easier since I thought I'd be at the hospital most of the time."

"You did what was necessary to get her the help she needs. Don't worry about the small things." He squeezed her hand. "She's sleeping now, so why don't we go get your stuff. You can check out and won't have to worry about doing it when she's discharged. That way, if she's tired, you can get her to the house, and into bed quickly. My appointments should be finished before the testing is complete, so whenever she's discharged I can lead the way to the house and you can follow me in your car."

She looked down the hall, toward Destiny's room, before she finally nodded. "Okay, let me just check on her."

"I'll let the nurses know. They have my cell number posted on the board and I'll tell them to call if she wakes up." He rubbed his thumb over the top of her hand in small circles. "Everything is going to be fine. She's going to get through this."

"I hope so." Her voice stayed low as if she worried that if she said it too loudly she might jinx it.

He wasn't sure how he knew, but things were going to work out. Destiny's cancer wasn't as bad as some of the cases he had seen. It was nasty, but not the worst, and there was no one better than Kingsley to help cure her.

Brian would be there to help every step of the way, because he'd be damned if he'd let her care fall below the best. It was something he could do in the memory of Jim, but it wasn't just for him, it was for Destiny and Nora too.

Twenty minutes later, Brian pulled up in front of the motel. Nora hadn't been kidding when she said it was close to the hospital. It was within walking distance, but it was also in a rather dangerous part of town. They passed a drug deal going down at the entry and countless other illegal activities in the last two blocks. What had she been thinking when she settled here?

"Don't start." She shook her head at him when he shoved the car into park and glanced her way. "I know what you're thinking. Since I'm never here, it didn't matter that the area was questionable."

"But when you *are* here…" He couldn't stop himself, because he knew Jim would be irate at the very idea of his wife living in this area and putting herself at risk.

"I know, but I'm never here. I've rarely left the hospital. This has mostly served as somewhere to keep our stuff. It's cheaper than a storage unit and close to the hospital. My only concern has been with

Destiny. This just seemed like a necessary evil." She moved to open the door, then stopped. "Now unless you wish to hang around in this neighborhood much longer, I suggest we grab my belongings and be on our way. I don't want to leave Destiny long."

He shook his head in resignation. "I won't hear of you finding a place to live in this neighbor, so don't even think about it."

Once they both closed their doors, he locked the car—not that there was much use to it. If anyone wanted to break in, they'd just smash the windows. He pocketed the keys and scanned the area again. "Why don't I begin loading the car and you go check out?"

She nodded and held out the room key. "Most everything is packed, what isn't I'll gather in a few minutes. It's room three." She nodded to one of the two doors they'd parked in front of.

He watched her walk to the office before striding toward the door. As he did, he questioned his decision not to go with her. It was his instinct to protect her, make sure that she was safe, but he also wanted to get them out of this area as quickly as possible. He turned the key and stepped inside.

The room was pretty bare, only two twin beds, a small table by the window, and a television stand pressed up against the wall. Next to the stand were three suitcases, and there were a few boxes closer to the bed. To see Nora's life packed into those few things tore at his heart.

He remembered moving around every few years with his family, and so many things got left behind. There was only one cherished belonging he still had from his childhood—a stuffed gorilla. To some it seemed unmanly to keep a stuffed toy, but he could still remember the day his grandfather bought it for him. It had been the only sentimental thing his grandfather had ever done. So, to this day, it sat on the chair in the master bedroom, a daily reminder of why he had chosen medicine as a career.

He grabbed two of the suitcases and turned to take them out, only to find Nora standing in the doorway. "What is it? Something wrong?"

"No, you seemed lost in thought and I didn't want to disturb you."

He glanced around the room one last time before turning back to her. "Seeing your belongings all packed up reminded me of my childhood. My father was an Army doctor, but you already know that, moving every few years was a way of life my whole childhood and this reminded me of it. To see your life reduced to what can fit into the back of your car, reminds me of us having to trim down our belongings every move because of the weight limit of household belongings the military would transport. We couldn't get rid of Mom's huge box of curtains because we never knew what size windows we'd have at our next place, but toys we hadn't played with or clothes we didn't wear were always donated."

"I never had to deal with a military move. Jim was killed before we got our next orders." Her voice hitched.

"I'm sorry. I didn't think." He sat the bags down and wrapped his arm around her shoulders.

"It's been over six years. I've grieved for him and I'm used to being alone. Everything with Destiny…it's just too much. For the first time, I feel so alone."

"You're not alone." He pulled her closer, wrapping both arms around her. "I'm here."

She looked up at him, her face just inches away from his, and he wanted to close the distance between them and claim her lips.

What the hell am I thinking? Whether he's dead or not, this is Jim's wife.

Chapter Five

Nora looked up at him, their gazes locked, and she wondered what the heck she was doing. There she stood in the arms of her deceased husband's best friend about to kiss him. This was wrong on so many levels. She felt his warm breath on her skin and her body urged her to lean forward. Over six years was too long to go without the comforting touch of a man; she craved it.

"We shouldn't." The words came out softer and with less authority than she had anticipated.

"I know." He agreed but didn't move away. "Just like I know I shouldn't do this." He caressed along her back, drawing her closer to his chest.

"Brian."

"You're beautiful." He lowered his head until their foreheads were touching.

"Please." She wasn't sure what she was asking for. For him to please kiss her? Please stop? Nevertheless, the sensation of someone's arms around her again was like Heaven.

He leaned back, his arms still around her but not as snuggly as before. "I apologize. This is a difficult enough time for you, you don't need this as well." He let his arms fall away from her and picked up the bags.

She stood there in the middle of the crummy motel room feeling more alone than ever before. She missed and longed for his touch, those soft caresses. It made her feel like she wasn't the only one in this whole uphill battle against cancer.

She wanted to curse her body for reacting to his touch; it was a betrayal in the most intimate way. With a deep breath she grabbed a box and headed to the car. She needed to get the stuff out of the room so she could get back to the hospital. It would put distance between them at least until tomorrow. Hopefully once she was at the house, he'd be working, she'd be looking for a rental, and when they were forced together Greta and Destiny would act as a buffer. No more intimate moments.

"I can get these. Why don't you check for anything that's not packed?" He took the box from her and loaded it onto the back seat.

"Who do you think loaded them into the car in the first place?"

"I have no doubt you can do it. I only suggested that you didn't have to." He shut the car door. "You know me, I'm a true southern gentleman. I don't like to see woman carrying heavy things. I open doors, pull out chairs, the whole nine yards."

She remembered that about him. The sweet way he made sure others were comfortable and how he would go out of his way to help. There had always been something about Brian that made her hope he would find the right woman, because he'd make a wonderful husband and father. Why he hadn't been snatched up years ago, she didn't know.

The hour was late and the hospital was as peaceful as it could get. Nora sat with her legs curled up under her, next to her daughter's bed, holding the last picture taken just hours before Jim deployed for the last time. Technically it was a picture of the three of them because she had been pregnant but hadn't known it. The only one of its kind. Her thoughts turned to what her husband would have said if he knew she had almost kissed Brian.

"You'd have a fit." She ran her thumb over the picture. *Only because if he was still alive I'd still be married.*

Now she was alone, a widow. He wasn't there and it was time to move on. That didn't mean she was moving on with Brian, or any other man right now, but her body was making it clear it had demands as well. She was focused on being a mother, but she had her own needs as well. She wasn't sure when, but eventually she'd have to embrace the woman within that she had smothered when she lost her husband.

When she decided it was time, it couldn't be with Brian. He had been Jim's best friend, and to her, he was off-limits. They could be friends, but she couldn't let things go any further. Not only because of Jim, but also for the sake of her daughter. *Stay focused.*

"Mommy…" Destiny rolled over onto her side.

"What is it, sweetie? Is your stomach upset again?" She set the picture back on the bedside table and leaned forward.

"Where did you go?"

"I went to get the stuff from the hotel. Tomorrow we're going to blow this joint and then on Friday we're going to go swimming." She touched the back of her hand to her daughter's forehead just to make sure there was no fever.

"Really?" Destiny pulled her teddy bear closer to her chest.

"Yep. We're going to stay with an old friend of mine. He's a doctor here and he has a pool in his house. Won't it be nice to get out of here?"

"Can we have pizza then?" The little girl's eyes glistened.

"Sure we can, anything you want." She tucked the blanket around Destiny. "Now get some sleep."

"Mommy, what about my sickness? Am I all better?"

"Not yet, sweetie." It pained her to say it but she wouldn't lie to her daughter. "Doctor Mathews is going to make you all better. One more day here while they run a few more tests and then we break free."

"Then I'll be all better?"

"Then next week you'll start getting medicine to make you feel better." She pushed the brown wavy locks away from her daughter's face. "Sleep, sweetie. I'll be right here."

With Destiny settled back down, her eyes fluttering shut again, Nora leaned back in the chair and tried to swallow the fears that were once again rising within her. She knew what she had told her daughter made it sound easier than it actually was, but when explaining it to a child she had to keep it simple. There was no need to tell her all the rough spots that might be ahead. Since Destiny couldn't remember how bad it was the last time, she needed to keep it upbeat. It was all part of motherhood for her to keep her worries and fears to herself. Plus, she was worried enough for the both of them.

She tried to calm herself with the thought that Doctor Mathews and Brian were both confident this treatment would work. Right now she had to put her faith in them. They had the medical knowledge to know the best course of action and it was up to her to trust them. She knew Brian; it might have been years since they had last talked, but he wouldn't tell her to do the experimental treatment if he wasn't confident it would work.

"Mrs. Horton." A nurse popped her head around the corner. "I wanted to let you know that Destiny's only allowed water until after the blood work is drawn."

"When will that be?"

"Should be around seven this morning since it has to be an eight hour fast. She'll get a later breakfast." The nurse turned to look down the hallway at someone stepping off the elevator before turning back to Nora. "If you need anything, just let me know. Otherwise, Doctor Mathews's orders are to let her sleep through the night. He wants her well rested for the exam tomorrow."

"Why?" Normally the nurses were in and out throughout the night, checking vitals, so to leave them undisturbed was unusual.

"I wouldn't be the right one to answer that. I'm normally in the emergency room, but they're short staffed so I've been rotated up. I can get one of the usual floor nurses to stop by and let you know."

Nora shook her head. "It's not important. A good night sleep for both of us sounds good to me."

"Okay. Would you like me to shut the door so the noise from the hall won't disturb you?"

"That would be nice. Thank you."

The very idea of sleeping without someone popping in and out all night sounded amazing, but what was even better was the knowledge that the next night she'd be in a comfortable bed. No more hospital recliner for her. Pure Heaven, even if that meant it would be in the same house with a man her body longed for but couldn't have—Brian.

Chapter Six

Brian leaned against the counter in the doctor's lounge with a cup of coffee in hand. It was long past lunch and this was the first break he'd managed to squeeze in. The day had brought one thing after another, with two emergencies thrown at him first thing that morning. One last patient to see and then he needed to find Nora. His thoughts had been trailing back to Nora and Destiny every chance he got. All he knew was the tests had ended almost two hours ago, and he was only privy to that because he'd bumped into Kingsley. Destiny's discharge papers were ready but they were waiting in her room for him. For the first time in his career he couldn't wait to get out of the hospital.

"Just the person I wanted to see." Brian's brother, Jason, stepped into the lounge.

"What's gone wrong now?" He set the coffee aside and tried to prepare himself for yet another kink in his plan to get out of there early.

"I wanted to talk to you about your newest house guests. What the hell are you thinking?" Jason stood next to Brian and poured himself a cup of coffee before diluting it with the vanilla creamer he favored.

"Don't start."

"How can I not? What are you thinking inviting a stranger into your home?"

"She's not a stranger, she's Jim's w…widow." He had almost said wife, but after the thoughts he'd had about her the night before he wanted to make it clear he wasn't doing anything wrong. The woman was a widow. Yes, she was his best friend's wife, but Jim wasn't here any longer. Maybe there was no one better than him to watch over her. Or at least that's what he'd convinced himself of last night.

"You haven't seen her in over six years. You didn't even know Jim was dead, or that they had a child. People change, yet you're going to invite her to live with you. Are you out of your mind?"

"Not her." He spoke with enough authority that Jason just looked at him, his eyes wide. "I couldn't just do nothing. If things were the other way around, I know they'd have done the same. Nora and Destiny deserve a few days outside of the hospital before the treatments begin. They're going to stay with me, end of story. I have the room and I want them there."

Jason set his coffee down with a thump and shook his head. "You're attracted to her."

"What?"

"You heard me. Tell me I'm wrong and I won't say another word." When Brian didn't deny it, Jason nodded. "I'm right. That's why you invited her to stay with you."

"I invited her because it's the right thing to do. Now there's nothing more to say on this." Brian grabbed the folders he'd placed on the counter and turned to leave.

"That woman is going through enough right now. I don't think it's wise for you to get involved."

"I'm already involved." He strolled out of the lounge without another word. He'd check on the last patient and then find Nora. What he wouldn't do was let Jason make him doubt what he was doing. Jason was the older brother and the two of them had always looked out for each other, but right now Brian didn't need that.

Once he got them out of the hospital and back to the house, the pressure would be off. There wouldn't be anyone around watching them intently, wondering what was happening between them. He could catch up on old times with her and begin to get to know her again. Damn, he couldn't wait to have her alone, without the distractions of the hospital.

Even as his thoughts twirled around her, he reminded himself that he couldn't have a relationship with her. Not with how he'd left things with Jim. She deserved someone better than him, someone like the man Jim was. He'd be there for her as a friend, maybe even a surrogate father to Destiny, but nothing more.

Twenty minutes later he finally stepped off the elevator, heading toward Destiny's room. As he neared, soft giggles escaped the room, mixing with Nora's voice. They were in high spirits today because they were being released from this prison.

"Excuse me, there's none of that in a hospital." He teased from the doorway, watching as Nora tickled Destiny's feet and the little girl wiggled around in the bed.

"Mommy." The little girl squealed.

"Oh, Brian, come in." Nora turned to him and smiled. "Destiny, this is Doctor West, he's the friend of mine that I told you we'd be staying with for the next few days."

"Where's his white coat?" She scooted up to the edge of the bed and eyed him with reservation.

"I left it in my office since I'm off duty, but if you'd like to see the proof I can take you there." He stepped into the room and placed his hands on the foot rail of the bed. "How about my hospital badge? Is that enough proof for you?" He held out the badge to her.

She looked at it and then at him. "Are you going to poke me again?"

"Poke?" He looked to Nora.

"She means the needles. There's been lots of blood work and other testing done today. She's tired of all of the jabs," Nora explained.

"Oh, no, sweetie. I'm just here to see if you're ready to go. I'm not here as a doctor." He clipped his badge back onto the pocket of his dress shirt. "To prove it, you can call me Brian instead of Doctor West."

"I'm hungry and Mommy said we could get pizza."

"Did she?" He glanced at Nora who was busy putting the last remaining things in a suitcase. "I think we can arrange for you to have the best pizza you've ever dreamed of having."

"Mmm, pizza." She bounced on the bed.

"You feed that girl pizza and she's yours forever. It's the way to her heart."

How about a way into her mother's heart? He swallowed the thought before he opened his mouth and ended up inserting his foot there. "Well, Greta makes a pizza that most would give their right arm for."

"Oh no, we can stop by somewhere. I don't want to put Greta out." Nora handed Destiny her coat.

He chuckled. "Greta's called twice today to find out what Destiny wanted for dinner. So you'd be putting her out if you wanted to order something. She's excited to cook for people, and that I'm going to be home at a reasonable hour."

"Who's Greta?" Destiny slipped her arms into her coat and picked up her teddy bear.

"She's a good friend of mine. She lives at my house too and kind of keeps things tidy."

"So, like a Mommy. She's your mommy." She jumped off the bed and came over to him.

"Greta is his housekeeper, not his mother." Nora shut the suitcase. "Are you ready, sweetie?"

When the little girl nodded, he stepped around her, and placed his hand over Nora's on the suitcase. "I'll take that."

She gave him a light laugh and nodded. "Fine, I'll grab the smaller one."

"Mommy, will I have to come back here?" Destiny grabbed a pillow from the edge of the bed and tucked it under her arm.

"Sweetie, remember, we talked about this last night. We'll be coming back every day for you to get medication to make you all better, but if everything goes okay you won't have to stay the night anymore."

"When do we come back?"

"In a few days." She took hold of her daughter's hand. "Ready?"

The little girl nodded and both of them turned to look at him. "I'm at your disposal," he said, grabbing the bag and walking toward them. "Where are you parked?"

"Near the front of the hospital."

"Then how about you ladies come with me? The doctor's parking lot is closer, that's where my car is, and we'll drive around the building to your car. That way you can follow me back to the house."

Nora nodded and they left the room. When they neared the nurses' station, Carly stepped around the counter and squatted before Destiny.

"I heard you were going home today and I'm glad I caught you because I have something for you." The nurse reached into her pocket and pulled out a small star keychain. "When I was a little girl I was sick just like you, so I had a keychain just like this. I put it around my stuffed animal and every time I had to be jabbed or didn't feel good, I would rub it."

"Did it make you feel better?"

"Not right away, but every night I'd make a wish. You know how you're supposed to make a wish upon a star in the sky? Well, I'd do the same thing with this and eventually I got better."

"You're all better now?" Destiny touched the keychain, her thumb glided over the smooth silver star.

Carly nodded. "I haven't been sick in a very long time. Now I want you to have it. If you do just what I told you, I know you'll be better, too."

"Really?"

"Yes. Doctor Mathews and the rest of us here are going to do our part. Will you do yours?" She held out the keychain.

"I will." Destiny nodded and took the keychain. "Will I see you again?"

"Yes. I'll still be here, and I'll make sure of it."

Destiny wrapped her arms around Carly's neck and kissed her cheek. "Thank you."

"Come on, sweetie." Nora laid her hand on her daughter's shoulder.

"I'll see you again real soon," Carly told her as Destiny slipped her arm from around her neck. "You be good for your mom."

Brian had watched the exchange silently. Carly was new there, and young; she cared for the patients, but that could burn her out in the long run. She showed a compassion some of the other nurses had hardened from over the years. This ward was more challenging than some of the others in the hospital, and saw more rotation with the nurses because of it.

Carly was good with Destiny, and he was sure she was with the other children, he just hoped it didn't burn her out quicker. They needed more nurses like her, who took the time to give an encouraging word to a child in need. Touched and filled with hope for the future, Brian walked with the two ladies out of the hospital and into the parking garage.

Chapter Seven

Nora opened the car door, stood, and looked up at the large two story brick house. It was beautiful and grand with thick white pillars in front. Trees surrounded the house on all sides, while still allowing plenty of open space.

"Mommy, look at the deer!"

"I see, sweetie." Even after looking to where her daughter was pointing, she couldn't keep her attention from the house. She looked back toward the front door as an older woman with short brown hair stepped outside.

"You're finally here." She came down the steps, heading straight to Destiny. "Aww, what a cutie you are. I'm Greta, and you must be Destiny."

The little girl nodded. "That's Mommy."

Nora came around the car. "I'm Nora. It's nice to meet you."

"You too. Now if I could steal your little girl away for a bit, I have a welcome treat for her." Greta held out her hand.

"Mommy, can I?"

Nora paused, looking between Greta and her daughter. "Okay, but don't cause any trouble. I don't want you spoiling your dinner, either."

"Just a little snack to welcome her." Greta winked at the little girl. "Then she can help me with the pizza."

"Behave," she warned her daughter as the two of them headed back into the house.

"Now that she has you two, I've been completely ignored," Brian teased. "I guess that leaves us to bring the stuff in."

"Greta seems nice and motherly. I bet you catch hell with your long hours."

"More than you know." He nodded and grabbed the suitcases he'd set aside. "She's been so excited about the two of you staying here. She loves kids and has even offered to watch her while you search for an apartment if you'd like. Not that there's any rush on that."

She reached into the car and grabbed Destiny's pillow and stuffed animal that she'd left behind. "I know you want to get back to your life. You don't want us hanging around. I checked the paper this morning and left a message about one. We'll have to wait to see when they call me back. The other two I called about were already taken."

"Places around here go fast...and I'm serious, there's no rush. Now let me show you around." He headed up the steps to the front door, leaving her no choice but to follow.

She still wasn't sure how to handle him or this forbidden attraction she had toward him. Their near kiss the night before still weighed on her mind, but it seemed as if he had forgotten. There was no uncomfortable mess or unease between them, but she couldn't stop thinking about it.

Part of her wished they had kissed, then the tension wouldn't have been there. She could have written it off as a mistake and moved on. Now, it seemed like yet another thing she'd let slip through her fingers. A near miss.

She wanted to feel his hands on her again, caressing up her back, just holding her. She longed for the comfort, not just the sexual side of things. She never realized how much she had missed it until suddenly she had it again but it was forbidden. It held so much more desire since it was a temptation she knew she had to deny.

Settled into their temporary accommodations, Nora set out a few of Destiny's toys, doing her best to make the place feel like home. She wasn't sure how long they'd be there, but she wanted her daughter to be able to play with whatever she wanted. The few days before the treatments started, they were going to try to forget about the cancer and just be normal.

"Mommy." Destiny came running into the room. "Greta showed me the pool. Can we go swimming now?"

"Not tonight, sweetie." She sat one of the baby dolls she'd unpacked onto the chair. "You had a busy day already so we're going to take it easy tonight. We're going to have pizza and then I'll put a movie on for you."

Destiny went to the bed and grabbed her teddy bear. "Is this my room?"

Nora nodded. "I thought you would like the purple comforter. The bathroom is across the hall. I've taken the room next to this, unless you want me to stay with you."

"I'm a big girl. I can sleep all by myself," her little girl stated proudly. "The bed matches my pillow."

"I know." She smiled. Purple was Destiny's favorite. A few months before her daughter got sick, they had painted her bedroom in a pale lavender to accent the purple and white design. It was one of the saddest parts of having to sell the house because it was the first sign her baby was growing up.

"There you are." Brian stood in the doorway. "Destiny, there's someone here to see you."

"Me?" She placed her bear on the bed. "Who?"

"Doctor Mathews and his wife."

"Doctor Mathews?" Nora's voice cracked and the worst thoughts ran through her mind. Had they found something else on the test results? Did Destiny no longer qualify for the study? Did that mean she'd have to go back to the hospital?

Brian stepped away from the doorway and went to Nora. He wrapped his arm around her shoulder, squeezing her gently. "It's a social visit, don't worry."

"Social for you, maybe, but why does he want to see Destiny?"

"Sweetie, why don't you go ahead downstairs? Your mom and I will be down in a moment." He waited until the little girl practically skipped from the room before he turned back to Nora. "His wife, Chelsea, lost her daughter to cancer a few years ago. In her memory, she started a charity—Hope's Toy Chest. It started out delivering presents to children at Cedar Grove for Christmas, and has expanded. This past Christmas the two of them helped a parent put together a Christmas celebration for her daughter a few weeks early because she wasn't expected to make it. Chelsea takes toys to children who just need a pick-me-up."

"I don't understand. Why are they here?"

"You left most of your stuff behind to move here and get Destiny the best care. Chelsea wanted to drop a few toys off for her to play with. Before you say it, I had nothing to do with it, this was Kingsley's idea. It will give her something new to play with."

She looked at the few things she'd put out for Destiny and nodded. Space in the car was limited and toys weren't the top priority when they were packing. They were only able to take her favorite things, and even that was inadequate. "You said Hope's Toy Chest was started in memory of her daughter…"

"Hope, she passed away a few years ago." He ran a hand down the length of her arm. "Don't think about it. Destiny is going to be okay. We're going to get through this."

"There are no guarantees in life."

"I know." He pulled her around to the front of him. "Destiny is going to beat this. She did it once before and she's going to do it again."

"I hope so." She blinked the tears away. "I don't know how I'd go on without her."

"You're not going to have to think about that because you won't have to. Trust me, she's going to pull through this and she'll be stronger than before." He kissed her forehead. "What do you say, shall we go downstairs?"

She nodded and he took her hand. "This is sweet of them but they didn't have to do something like this. I'm sure there are plenty of others who need it more."

"This is what Chelsea does. It's kept her sane and helped her get over the loss of her daughter. She just recently agreed with Kingsley to bring on someone to help her and that's only because she found out she was pregnant."

"Pregnant, that's wonderful." She remembered how joyous it was when she found out she was pregnant with Destiny. Even after the news came that Jim had been killed, being pregnant was the one thing that kept her going.

"They married almost a year ago and have been trying for several months. They just found out a few weeks ago and she's due at the end of September. She wants to train someone she trusts before she's too far along. With her due date so close to the busy season for Hope's Toy Chest, she wants to make sure whoever she brings on to help is able to handle it," he explained on their way downstairs.

"Sounds like it will be a busy time for her. A new baby, the holidays, the charity, it will keep her on her toes."

"I'm not sure if Chelsea knows any other way." He chuckled. "It seems like every few months she's got an idea to make the charity better than it was before."

"It sounds like a great organization." She had been involved in charity work before her daughter was born. It was mostly visiting injured military personnel at the hospital, talking with their families, making sure their needs were met, and sending care packages. She had been very involved with her husband's platoon and had made the most out of military life. It had been a way to ease the loneliness.

But when Jim was killed, that ended. All the friends she had were military spouses and they seemed to fall away after she moved off base. Their lives were different. The months before Destiny's birth had been the longest and loneliest time in her life. It was sad that with Jim's death she'd lost so much more than just her husband.

"Mommy, Mommy, look." Destiny hollered to her the moment they came around the corner to the living room where everyone had gathered. She held up a big purple stuffed dog with white spots. "It's a message dog. There are these markers and you can draw or write all over him. Then you throw him in the wash to clean him, so you can do it all over again."

"Wow, and he's your favorite colors. Did you say thank you?"

Destiny nodded and uncapped one of the pens to start doodling on her dog.

"Hello, I'm Chelsea. I hope you don't mind the impromptu visit, but I thought Destiny might like a few new toys to keep her busy."

"It's very kind of you, thank you." She looked around, suddenly unsure what she should do.

"Nora, you okay?" Brian touched her arm.

"Sorry, normally I'd offer a guest a coffee or something, but as I'm a guest here I'm not sure what to do. It's the southern heritage in me." Everyone shared a good laugh while she began to feel slightly at ease.

"Mommy, Greta's doing that. Come play with me." Destiny sat on the floor, playing with her new toys.

"In a bit, sweetie. We have visitors and I'm going to talk with the grown-ups for a bit."

"How about we all have a seat?" Brian suggested. "There's no reason we should stand around the entryway."

"We can't stay long." Chelsea was interrupted by Greta, who walked in carrying a tray full of drinks. "I know you're still trying to get settled, but if there's anything I can do please don't hesitate to call. If you need someone to talk to, there's a call list."

"Call list?"

"My wife's newest project, because she doesn't have enough on her plate." Kingsley smiled at Chelsea as he rubbed the back of her hand with his thumb.

"You should have received the list in your check-out folder."

"She did," Kingsley assured her before looking to Nora. "I put it in there, along with some additional paperwork on the treatment in case you wanted to look it over again. My cell number is on the top of the first page if any questions arise that Brian can't answer."

"I haven't had a chance to look over the folder yet, it was on my plans for after Destiny went to bed."

"There's no rush," Chelsea said. "I just wanted to let you know there's a list in there. Two different columns, one with parents who are going through treatments now and the second list is with parents whose children are in remission. Any of them are willing to talk, or you can call me anytime. My number is also on the bottom."

"It's sweet, all you're doing for us. Brian told me a little about your charity, I think it's wonderful. Before Destiny was born I was active in charity work, and would love to get involved again. I won't know if I can until I see how the treatments go, but if I can be of any help please let me know." She hadn't planned to offer her services, but maybe in the future once things were settled, and she had a place of her own, she might be able to help. Knowing how much Chelsea did for people, Nora couldn't stop herself. She suddenly realized she had committed herself without giving it proper thought.

Then again, maybe helping out could decrease her worry. She doubted it, because late at night when the world was sleeping she was always awake worrying. It had been her trademark when her husband was deployed, and it carried over with Destiny. Every ounce of her was a worrier, and that wasn't likely to change anytime soon.

Destiny's Wish: Cedar Grove Medical

Chapter Eight

The rest of the day had gone by in a flash and smoother than Nora thought it would. Destiny had quickly settled into Brian's house and gave her no problems at bedtime. Her little girl was excited to be able to sleep in a real bed again by herself and not have her mother sitting in a chair by her bedside all night.

Nora wasn't sure what to do with herself. It was too early to go to bed. What they needed for the next few days while she was looking for an apartment had already been unpacked, so she felt lost and uneasy. She wandered around the house, unable to sit still.

"Nora," Brian called out as she strolled past his office. He had gone there earlier to check on an email while she put Destiny to bed.

"Sorry, I didn't mean to disturb you. I was only——"

"Wearing a line in the hardwood floor?" he supplied with a smirk. "Come in here and tell me what's got you on edge. Was it something I've done?"

She stepped into the doorway of his office, but didn't enter. "How could it be you? You've been nothing but wonderful and generous."

"Then why don't you tell me what has you pacing the house? Are you worried about Monday?"

"How can I not be? Any parent would be." She wrapped her arms around her middle, holding herself so she didn't fall apart again. "I'm sorry I'm so emotional. One minute I think everything is going to work out, but then the next I question things again. I'm just a mess right now."

"Which is why I came in here to check for this email." He rose from behind the desk and came toward her. "I got someone to cover my rounds at the hospital and any emergencies that might arise. That means I'm off until Monday and I was thinking we should go away for a few days. My parents have a cabin a little over an hour from here, it's in the middle of nowhere. We could let Destiny swim in the morning and then after lunch we could slip out of town for a few days and forget about next week. It's high in the mountains, so I'm sure there's still snow on the ground."

"I'm supposed to be looking for an apartment."

"You can do it when we get back. A weekend out of the city is just what you need. We'll take some board games and movies to keep us entertained. I think a trip like this is just what we all need. We can give her a few days of normal."

"What happens if something goes wrong? If she gets sick?" Anxiety sparked within her.

"Hmm." He rubbed his jaw. "I guess if you had a doctor with you, that might help. Wonder where you can find one of those?"

She gave him a light slap on his arm. "Being a smart ass never suited you very well."

"I'm being serious. You should have a doctor with you for Destiny's sake, after all, anything could happen. Give me a minute and I'll think of something." His eyes twinkled with amusement.

"Okay, so I wasn't thinking and I'm being an overprotective mother. What do you want from me?"

He took hold of her hand and pulled her against him. "You're not overdoing it, you're just being a good mother. I'll be there, and if anything changes in her condition we'll come back straight away. I think you need this break as much as she does, so what do you say?"

She nodded. "Okay, but what about Greta? She asked Destiny to help her bake cookies tomorrow."

"Don't worry about Greta, she's not going to let us slip out of here without her. She loves going to the cabin and there's plenty of room there for all of us. My parents added on to the old cabin a few years ago expecting it would be somewhere we could all gather, with grandbabies running around."

"Do you go a lot?"

"Not as much as any of us would like. With our schedules, it's hard for us to get away. Three of us gone from the hospital at the same time and everything."

"Three?" She leaned back out of his embrace to look up at him.

"I believe I told you that Jason is a pediatric surgeon and Elizabeth is a grief counselor at the hospital, so they both have active careers. They also adopted a beautiful little girl, Faith, and she's about to turn a year old on Valentine's Day. My parents' first grandbaby, and boy do they spoil her rotten already."

"As her uncle, are you saying you don't have anything to do with that?" She smirked. "The first child born into a family is one everyone dotes on. I've seen how you are with Destiny. I have no doubt you're guilty of spoiling Faith."

"Never." He tried to hide a smile but failed miserably. "I'm a doctor, I know how disastrous it can be to spoil a child. I would have no part in making my niece a brat."

"Not all spoiled children are brats. Look at Destiny, I do my best to spoil her, to make up for what she doesn't have, and what she's gone through. She's not a brat, or at least I hope others don't think she is."

He rubbed small circles along her back. "She's a great kid, with manners, and respect. Though I'll say she acts older than she is, but that's because of all she's been through. She needs this break as much as you do. Let her be a kid again. We can eat popcorn, watch movies, do all the things she loves to do. Whatever that is."

"It doesn't sound like much fun for you," she reasoned, as she toyed with the button on his dress shirt.

"It will be because I'll be with you and Destiny. What do you say?"

"Let's do it." She gave in to the temptation to get away and give her daughter some normalcy. "We can leave after lunch and Destiny can take her nap in the car. Since she's been sick she's been sleeping a lot more. Afternoon naps are a must."

"We can wait until she wakes up."

"No, it's fine, she sleeps during car rides anyway. We don't want her to get two naps in, one before we leave and another one in the car, otherwise I'll have problems getting her to sleep at bedtime." She let her fingers move toward the edge of his shirt, where it opened up to his skin. "After all, grown-ups need time to themselves, too."

"That they do." He brought his hands down to rest on her hips. "Come sit."

"Something wrong?"

"No." He kept his arm around her waist and directed her toward the small sofa in his office. "It's been years since we've seen each other, I thought maybe we could catch up. Six years is too long."

"There's not much to catch up on. Being a single mother, my life has revolved around Destiny. There's not much time for anything else."

"You've had to be doing something all these years." He pulled her down onto the sofa next to him and placed his arm around her shoulders, holding her tight. "What about work?"

"Jim and the military made sure that if something happened I'd be financially secure but for the last three years I've been a virtual assistant for a marketing firm, mostly writing press releases, following up on details for events, little things like that. It allowed me to be home with Destiny."

"Why did you quit?"

She leaned into his embrace, resting her head against his shoulder. "My boss didn't give me much of a choice. She needed someone to attend an upcoming event and I couldn't, not with Destiny's health. I hated to hand in my resignation but my daughter had to come first. I met a lot of people through that job who will be friends for a lifetime."

"I'm sorry things ended like that. You mentioned to Chelsea about helping with Hope's Toy Chest. Have you considered you could be just what she's looking for? Your marketing experience could be an advantage to bringing in more donations. She's always wanted to take Hope's Toy Chest to the next level, doing new things, bigger events. You could help her with that."

"Destiny…" She shook her head, but he cut her off before she could finish.

"Destiny is sick and sitting around worrying about it won't help her. Kingsley will be doing everything he can, all of us will. You need something for you, and I'm sure Chelsea will work with you so that you can be with Destiny." He caressed her shoulder gently. "Think about it. You want to get involved, and this might be a better fit for you than just volunteering with the charity."

"I'll admit it might be a good fit, but the timing is wrong. Destiny needs me, she has no one else."

"You're wrong there." He took her hand in his. "The two of you have me. I'm not going to let you go through this alone."

"You've already done so much for us." She placed her hand on his chest, her body curving against his. "Helping me get Destiny out of the hospital means everything to me. I'll never be able to repay you for that."

"No repayment is necessary."

His hand moved down her back. Soft, yet strong enough to let her know he was there. It wasn't a touch from just a friend, but from someone who clearly wanted more. Her stomach churned. "Brian, why are you doing this? Helping me, inviting me to stay here? Don't tell me it's because of Jim. He's been dead for over six years and I've been doing fine without him. More to the point, look where your hand is. You're not doing this because I'm his widow."

She watched as his gaze traveled down to where his hand rested on her stomach, just below her breast, his thumb brushing against the underside of her chest. "I—"

"Please don't lie to me."

He pulled his hand away and held onto the armrest of the sofa. "It started out in Jim's memory. Now…Nora, it's more than that, it's you."

"Me?" The spark of surprise shot through that single word.

"Yes. Woman, you're amazing. With everything that's happening, you still have things under control. You're focused, determined, and damn it, as much as I fight it…I want you."

"I don't feel like I'm in control. It seems like everything is spinning out of control and there's nothing I can do about it." She blinked. "What, what? *Want* me?"

"Did Jim ever tell you the story of the day we met you for the first time?" When she shook her head, he continued. "You were sitting at that café, your girly coffee off to the side as you worked on your laptop. Your hair was in a messy bun and that pale pink sweater fell off your shoulder, just enough to give a glimpse of the creamy skin hidden beneath. You were beautiful and I was going to ask you out, but he beat me to the punch. All these years, that has been my biggest regret. The only consolation I had was that the two of you were perfect together. You accepted him and his career, keeping the home front covered while he was overseas. There were times when I could see the loneliness in your eyes, but he'd never listen."

She remembered that loneliness and the sleepless nights. Sometimes it was so bad she thought her heart would break from the need to see him, to touch him. Every time she'd put enough distance between her heart and her husband so she could deal with the separation, he'd return only to leave again. Being a military spouse made her stronger, but it also made her lose a part of herself.

"The loneliness was rough, but I'd have done it a hundred times over to be with the man I fell in love with. It got worse when he changed. It seemed like every time he'd leave again, he'd come back and there was more distance between us. No matter how hard I worked, he wouldn't bridge the gap.He kept his walls firmly in place."

"Maybe he did that to protect you." He ran his hand down the length of her arm. "War changes people, as you've seen. He might have kept the barriers up so you wouldn't see the worst in him. After he started deploying, even I saw the changes in him. His temper was always boiling just below the surface. It's possible the walls were to protect you from that. Not because he didn't love you and still wanted you the same way he did when he married you."

"It's not that uncommon," she acknowledged. "Other spouses went through it as well, but most of them worked through it. Jim and I never got that chance. He volunteered for that deployment. I begged him not to. I knew his head wasn't in the right place."

She shook her head, unable to say that because he hadn't listened he had been killed. She tried not to wonder how things would have been if he hadn't volunteered for that deployment.

Would they still be married? At least then Destiny would have a father. More than anything, it was Destiny who was missing out.

Destiny's Wish: Cedar Grove Medical

Chapter Nine

In all the years Brian had lived in the house, he couldn't recall a time he actually enjoyed the pool as much as he did with Destiny around. Before, it had been a place to do his morning laps, constant upkeep for little reward. Now, as he tossed Destiny across the pool, he was glad he didn't give in to the temptation to close it up. Her giggles bounced off the walls and echoed throughout the closed space.

"Throw me again." She swam toward him.

"Okay, but this is the last time. Remember we promised your mom we'd be out before she came back with your lunch." He hooked his hands under her arms and hauled her out of the water.

"Mommy's a spoil sport." She complained as she got into position to launch herself from him.

"We'll swim again after we get back from the cabin," he told her, hoping he wasn't make a promise he wouldn't be able to keep. "Ready?" When she nodded, he lifted her higher and threw her across the pool where she landed with a splash just as the door opened and Nora rejoined them.

"I thought you promised to have her out before I returned." She stood at the edge of the pool, her hands on her hips as if she was mad, but the smile stretching across her face said otherwise.

"I can't help it if she's convincing." He scooped Destiny out of the water and put her on his shoulders. "Your mom is complaining, we better get out."

"Come on Mom, one more, please."

"No." She set the plate on the table and grabbed a towel. "Greta made you a sandwich with a little pasta salad on the side, and I want you to eat. If you're good we'll swim when we get back."

He lifted her over the edge of the pool where Nora wrapped a towel around her. "Remember, we're going to have lots of fun at the cabin so we need to get on the road. Go eat."

Nora secured the towel around Destiny before she looked down at him. "Once she's done eating, we'll take a quick shower to wash the chlorine off and then we're ready to hit road."

The door to the pool room opened. "Two more sandwiches," Greta announced, setting them on the table along with drinks. "How's lunch, sweetie?"

"Good." Destiny took another bite.

He climbed out of the pool and slung his arm around Nora's waist. "She loves the water. Are you sure she's not part fish?" They had been in the pool for over three hours, the longest he had ever used it.

"She'd spend all day in there if I'd let her, and turn into a shriveled prune." She shook her head and leaned back against him. "You're good with her."

"She's a great kid. Even with all she's going through she's laughing and have a good time. That's a good sign."

"She's going to sleep well in the car but when we get there she's going to be ready to go again." She tipped her head back to look up at him. "You sure you want to be locked in a cabin with her all weekend?"

"Not just her, but you and Greta. Though I have to admit I'm looking forward to being alone with you after she goes to bed." He kissed her temple.

He wasn't sure when it had happened, but somehow he'd let himself get drawn closer to her when what he should have been doing was keeping his distance. If he was serious about her, there was something she needed to know. She needed to know the real reason he hadn't been in touch since a few weeks prior to Jim's last deployment. *Tonight. I'll tell her tonight.*

The rest of the evening went smoothly, but Brian couldn't ease the tightness in his shoulders. Even with Destiny napping the whole two hour drive, she was still sleepy, making it easy for them to camp out in front of the television and watch movies. He hadn't been able to focus with his arm around Nora, the ball of tension in his stomach. He wasn't sure how she'd react when he finally came clean, but it was time to clear the air. Otherwise, he'd never be able to move forward with her—which was what he wanted most.

"Brian, did you hear me?" Nora stood by the edge of the sofa, having gathered the popcorn bowls and glasses.

"What?" He blinked, pushing his thoughts away.

"I asked you if you wanted anything. Greta's calling it a night, she's going to do some reading in bed, but wanted to know if you needed anything before she turned in."

"No, I'm fine." He tapped the seat next to him. "Come join me."

"Let me take these to her first." She disappeared into the kitchen before he could stop her, giving him another moment to gather himself.

He rose from the sofa and paced before the fireplace. The warmth from the fire helped ease the chill settling over him. He couldn't help but doubt his decision to tell her. The fight with Jim was in the past, it should stay there, but he couldn't move onward unless he came clean. They needed everything to be out there in the open.

"Greta sent these." Nora held up two glasses of red wine. "Drink, maybe that will loosen your tongue, and you can tell me what's on your mind."

"You're right. I did want to talk to you." He took the wine glass and took a sip. "I…" He let out an uneasy laugh, before shaking his head. "I give people bad news all the time, and it's nothing like telling you this."

"Just out with it." She set her wine glass on the coffee table and came to stand before him. "Whatever it is, it's best to get it out."

"Jim…"

She placed her hand on his chest. "Do we have to talk about him tonight? He seems like a constant ghost between us."

He laid his hand over hers, entwining their fingers. "That's why we need to talk. See, I hadn't been in touch for a number of weeks before Jim died and lost touch because of an argument we had when he put his name in for that deployment."

"What?"

"I couldn't believe Jim had volunteered for it, considering how much you needed him. I thought if I talked to him, maybe he'd see reason, but it only made things worse." He squeezed her hand. "I tried to tell you earlier but I chickened out."

"When?"

"When we were talking about the day we first met, and I said there were times when I could see the loneliness in your eyes but he'd never listen. Damn it, Nora, I knew you wanted him out of the Army and I tried to convince him of that. It was the biggest fight we had, and the next day he boarded that flight to Iraq. He was killed and I never got to make things right between us. He was a better man than I could ever be. He fought and died for this country, for all of us, and all I can think is he left you alone. You deserved better than that."

"I'm not the only war widow. We all deserve to have our husbands come back to us, but some of us aren't granted that luxury. He died to keep us safe at home. He's a hero…but you're right, there are times I hate him for it." She paused, took a deep breath, and let it out slowly. "Could I honestly say we'd still be married if he was here? I don't know. We were having problems when he left for that last deployment.

Maybe some of them were because of the deployment, but the bigger part was that he had changed. He wasn't the man I married. He was different, the war had altered him."

He wrapped his arms around her, holding her close, as tears streamed down her face. "I know, I saw the changes, too," he reminded her.

"I never stopped loving him, but I buried him years ago. Maybe it's time to move on."

He kissed the top of her head. "I was hoping you'd say something like that, but I needed you to know the real reason I had lost touch. I hated to stand by while the sadness in your eyes grew stronger and there was nothing I could do."

"I appreciate that you tried to talk to Jim. I tried, but he wouldn't listen. He said he needed to go and at the time I thought because he wanted to protect us back home. Now I wonder if he didn't go because he couldn't live with the man he'd become, the man who'd seen and did what he had to do in that war." She laid her head against his chest. "It's something we'll never know."

"No matter how it changed him, you have to know he never stopped loving you." He gently caressed her back.

"I do, and he gave me a beautiful daughter." She leaned back and looked up at him. "Brian, what's happening between us? It feels like more than just rekindling a friendship."

"I'm hoping it's more than just friendship because what I feel for you is beyond friendly. I want you, Nora." He lowered his head until his lips hovered just above his. "In every way imaginable and then some."

He closed the distance and claimed her lips. The spiciness of the wine hit him with full force as he let his tongue slip between her lips and explored the contours of her mouth. He ran the tip of his tongue over the sharpness of her teeth before she returned his kiss, bringing her tongue to meet his. With one final kiss he pulled away to look down at her.

"Come to bed with me."

She tilted her head, her long hair tickling the backs of his hands where they remained on her back. "That sounded like a bad pick-up line."

"Not a line at all. Plus, I hope I don't have to use bad pick-up lines. I think I already have you."

"Oh, Brian." She tried to pull back from him but he kept his arms around her waist. "I'm a widow, with a sick daughter, and no job. You deserve someone so much better."

"You're the woman I haven't been able to get out of my thoughts for years. As for the daughter, so what? As you said, I'm good with her, and she seems to like me. Isn't that what a single mothers wants, for her child to like the new man in her life?"

"It means everything that she likes you, but things aren't going to be easy with her treatments and everything. This isn't the time for you to get wrapped up in us."

"I already am." He cupped the side of her cheek. "I told you before I'm going to be with you through Destiny's treatments, and we'll get through this *together.*"

"You don't have to."

"I want to." His trailed his thumb along her cheekbone. "I want to be with you and Destiny. Don't push me away."

"I have no intention of pushing you away, I just wanted to give you fair warning that you should be running in the opposite direction."

"You won't catch me running anywhere unless it's toward the two of you." He rested his head against her forehead. "The next few months might be trying. Destiny is going to have good and bad days, but never doubt that I'm in this with you completely. You're not alone now."

"Thank you." A tear rolled down her cheek and he used his thumb to wipe it away.

"I didn't mean to make you cry." There was something about the tears that rolled down her cheeks that made him want to fight for her, fight so he'd never have to see another tear of sadness fall from her eyes again. She brought out an honor and goodness within him. He was falling in love with her.

Chapter Ten

Wrapped in Brian's arms, Nora wanted to say something to convince herself that what they were doing wasn't wrong. She wanted to push her doubts away, but they kept creeping back at the worst moments. He was her husband's best friend, shouldn't he be the one person who was off-limits?

She couldn't stop her body from reacting to him, her thoughts entangling themselves with him, and she couldn't stop this desire to be with him. She had never felt this way with anyone but Jim, and now he was gone. She couldn't be the lonely widow her whole life. Brian was just the man to change that.

"Mommy!" A screech tore through the house and through Nora's heart.

"Destiny." She stepped back out of his embrace and tried to push away the fears that were rising within her. She knew going so far from the hospital was a bad idea.

"Don't panic." He followed her toward Destiny's room. "It might be nothing."

"We're so far from the hospital if something's wrong."

"Little mother, it's going to be fine."

She pushed open the door to Destiny's room. "Sweetie, what is it?"

Greta peeked out of her bedroom. "Is everything okay?"

"Mommy, the light went out. It's dark." Destiny was curled up in the corner where her bed met the wall, hugging her teddy bear to her chest, tears running down her face.

"Everything's fine," he told Greta before stepping into the room behind Nora. "The light bulb just went out. I'll get another one." He pulled his cell phone from his pocket and turned on the flashlight application, holding it out to Destiny. "Here, sweetie, will this work until I can get the lamp fixed?"

Her little hand reached out and grabbed it. "Thank you."

Nora sat on the edge of the bed while Brian slipped out of the room to get the new bulb. "It's okay, sweetie, Brian will have a new light in the lamp in a few minutes. Why don't you lay back down?"

"I woke up and it was so dark." Destiny scooted down into the bed and Nora covered her. "I don't like it."

"I know, sweetie, you've gotten used to having the light from the hospital. It's hard to sleep in the dark and in a new place, but it's going to be okay." Her stomach started to calm, now that she knew her daughter was okay. Everything was going to be all right.

"I've got a new light bulb." Brian held it in his hand as he strolled across the room toward the lamp. "We'll have this room bright again in a few moments."

"I'm thirsty." Destiny pointed the flashlight toward where Brian was changing the light.

"If you're okay now, I'll get you a glass of water. Brian will you stay with her." She patted her daughter's arm.

"We'll be fine, go ahead." He twisted the new bulb into place and the room lit up. "How's that, sweetie, bright enough?"

Destiny nodded. "Thank you."

With one last glance at Brian, Nora rose from the bed and headed toward the door. She knew her little girl was safe with Brian even if all the lights in the house went out. He had comforted her with the flashlight and had come to her rescue, just like he had done with Nora. The knight in shining armor. Or rather, the doctor in the white lab coat.

With the light working again, Brian dug a little flashlight from his pocket and sat down on the edge of the bed. "Look what I have for you. It's a flashlight with a little arm strap, you can wear it around your wrist in case the lights go out again. Then you'll never be in the dark again." He held it out to her.

"Thank you." She reached out and took it, placing his phone in his hand in exchange for the miniature flashlight. Pressing the button on the end, she tested it to make sure it worked before slipping it around her wrist.

"You're welcome. Anything else I can get you?"

She twirled the flashlight between her fingers, her gaze locked on it. "A daddy."

Her voice was so low, he wasn't sure he caught what she was saying. His heart lurched into his throat. "What was that?"

"I want a daddy." She looked at him. "Mommy says if you wish upon a star your wish will come true. I've always wished for a daddy but I've never gotten one. Other girls have one."

"You do have a daddy, and he was a good man." He nodded to the picture of Jim and Nora that sat by the bed. "He's in Heaven watching over you."

"I want one that's here. I want one for Mommy. I've been so sick and she's been so sad, I want a Daddy to make her happy again. You make her smile and I like you." She looked up, turning her big green eyes on him. "Will you be my daddy?"

He took her small hand into his much larger one. "Sweetie, anyone would be honored to be your daddy. You're a bright little girl and we're going to make you all better soon."

"Then will you be my daddy?"

It pained him that she wanted him to say yes but he couldn't. He couldn't give hope when he wasn't sure what would happen between him and Nora. "That's not up to me. We need to see how things work out with your mom and me, but I'll always be there for you when you need someone."

"I need someone now. I need a daddy now," she demanded with intense determination. "There's a daddy daughter tea party at the hospital but I don't have a daddy to take me." She frowned, her bottom lip poking out.

"How about this, if your mom is okay with it I'll be your daddy for the day and take you to the tea party. What do you think?"

"Really?" She perked up.

"Yes, but your mom has to say it's all right." He patted her hand. "I'll talk to her and we'll see what she says."

"What who says?" Nora stepped into the room, a glass of water in her hand.

"Busted." Destiny smirked.

"Nothing." He winked at Destiny and stepped away from the bed so Nora could give her the water.

"What's this?" Nora questioned as Destiny reached up for the glass.

"My light."

"It's a miniature flashlight, in case the lights go out. She'll have something to use until we can get to her," Brian explained as he stepped closer to the door. "I'll wait for you in the living room."

Knowing that when Destiny had settled back down into bed, Nora would follow, he slipped away. It would give him a moment to get over her wish. The poor little girl wanted so much to have a dad. One who would do the things with her she'd seen other girls do. It was sweet and sad all at the same time. He could do the tea party and other activities with her, but he'd never replace Jim.

"You promised to go to the daddy and daughter tea party with her?" Nora strolled toward him but he wasn't sure if she was angry or not.

"Yes, but if you'd rather I didn't—"

"No." She went to him. "I think it's wonderful. Thank you. That tea party was something she's wanted to go to but I wasn't sure how to make it happen. They wanted only fathers for the event, since it's Valentine's Day."

"Come sit." He sat down on the sofa and patted the cushion beside him. She sat down beside him and he wrapped his arm around her shoulders. "Do you realize how much she wants a father of her own?"

"What?" She tipped her head towards him, her eyebrow raised.

"Destiny asked me to be her daddy. That she's wished on a star every night hoping to have one but even though you said it would, her wish never came true. She wants a daddy for you, too."

"For me?" Her eyes widened.

"She doesn't realize that her daddy wouldn't also be yours. She just wants someone to be there for you. With her being sick she knows you're worried and wants to make sure you're comforted. She thinks the two of you having a daddy will make you happy again."

"Oh, no." She shook her head. "I'll have to talk to her in the morning about this. I mean, I know she wanted a father but she can't just go around asking people."

"She didn't pick a stranger. She picked someone she knows makes her mom smile, someone her mom likes. I think in her own way,

Destiny has given you her blessing on what's happening between us. That's important, not only to you, but to me. I want her to be comfortable."

"Taking on a child is a lot. Most men would be running the other way from a single mother."

He cupped her chin and turned her head enough to look at him. "I'm not most men."

"No, you're not." She laid her hand on his leg. "You're amazing and so much more than I could have asked for. Especially with all that's happening."

"You're worrying again." He let go of her chin and laid his hand over hers.

She frowned. "Monday is looming and the closer it gets the more nervous I become. When I'm busy I can push it away from my thoughts, but in moments like this everything comes rushing back to me stronger than before."

"Well, I think we can find something to keep your mind off it."

She nuzzled her head closer to his neck. "What did you have in mind?"

"How about a dip in the hot tub? The hot water can ease your stress."

"That way you get to see me in my suit again." Her lips curled into a smile.

"Hey, this is for you. I'd have suggested a movie, cuddling in bed, but if you can't get into the movie than you'll just think about everything we're trying to get your mind off of."

"Hmm, I was thinking of something more fulfilling." She slid onto his lap, stradling him. "Something in bed, but it has nothing to do with a movie. Cuddling, sure, but no movie."

"Now, that I can arrange." He leaned forward and claimed her lips.

Sometime during the night, Nora had managed to fall into a deep sleep in Brian's arms and slept the rest of the night. It had been the first truly restful sleep she'd had since Destiny's cancer returned. Sleeping in the hospital recliner, with the nurses in and out all night, did nothing for her. If it wasn't the nurses waking her, there was some other kind of excitement. No matter how she'd tried, she had never managed more than a few hours' sleep.

She awoke more refreshed than she had in months. The sun was streaming through the windows, casting rays of light across the floor and the bottom of the bed. She rolled onto her back and stretched, enjoying the moment. The comfortable bed meant she didn't have kinks in her neck or back like she was used to. When his hand slipped across her waist she stilled for a moment, remembering everything that had happened the night before.

She wanted to curl back into his embrace where she was content, safe, but most importantly she'd found something she had been missing—love. What they had was special, almost perfect. It was more than she could have ever asked for. He was amazing with her daughter. *Love*. She was falling in love with him. Her heart fluttered until she thought it would fly away.

"Good morning, beautiful." He nuzzled closer to her and pressed his body along the length of hers.

"'Morning."

She glanced at him, grogginess still clinging to his features, his eyes half open. Her daughter's soft giggles drifted down the hallway from the living room.

She sat up against the headboard and glanced down at her thin white tank top. "I left my sweater in the living room."

"There's a robe on the back of the bathroom door, or you can take one my shirts."

"I've got a better idea, why don't I just stay in bed?" She slumped back down again, her head on the pillow.

He teased his fingers along the curve of her hip. "I think we can keep ourselves busy in here."

"What about Destiny?"

"There's always Greta. They're supposed to make cookies this afternoon together." He kissed her shoulder.

"Tempting, but I can't do that to Greta. When Destiny is feeling better she's got a lot of energy." She slipped out of his embrace and scooted to the edge of the bed. In doing so, she caught a glimpse of the alarm clock. Eight twenty-three in the morning. "I can't believe I slept this long!"

"I can, after last night." He smirked at her. "Tonight I plan for act two."

"Act two? I thought we had that around midnight." She rose out of bed, the cool air on her bare skin sending goosebumps racing along her body.

"I can't get enough of you, so I don't care what act it is, I want you now, tonight, and always."

She couldn't stop the smile from spreading across her face. "Mommy duties now, but in a few hours it will be nap time and I'm sure we can find something to occupy our time." She grabbed her jeans and bra before padding off toward the bathroom to get freshened up.

"I'll be ready," he called after her just as she shut the bathroom door.

She spun toward the mirror, laid her clothes on the counter, and caught a glimpse of herself. Her cheeks were blushed with a healthy glow; the dark circles that had been a constant feature were suddenly gone. It was amazing what a bout of lovemaking and a good night's sleep could do for a person.

But it was more than that. There was a glisten in her eyes, a smile that wouldn't dissipate, and her heartbeat fluttered every time she and Brian touched. She *knew* she was in love.

Chapter Eleven

The weekend went by much too quickly for Brian, and Monday morning arrived in a blink of an eye. Not only was he back to work at the hospital but it was time for Destiny's first treatment. His stomach roiled every time he thought about it. He had rearranged things so he could be with Nora and Destiny for the first treatment. It was likely they wouldn't notice any of the unfortunate side effects right away, but at least he'd be there for support and comfort. He cared not only for Nora but also for Destiny, and he was determined to be there for them. If there was anything he could do to help them through this journey, he would do it.

"Doctor West."

He turned at the sound of his name and found Nancy stepping off the elevator. "Hello, Nancy. What can I do for you?"

"I wanted to say thank you. I don't know what you did, but you got Nora and Destiny a place to stay so they could get out of this hospital. I don't understand it, but somehow the few days away from here gave Nora a brighter outlook. She's doesn't seem as gloomy and fearful as she was before. There's a smile on her face, and Destiny is giggling. They're like totally different people."

He wasn't sure what to say. He didn't mind anyone knowing that Nora was staying with him, but he wasn't sure how much she wanted everyone to know. "Being able to get away from the stress of the hospital can do a world of good for all of us."

"You seem in a rather chipper mood yourself."

"I am." He smirked. "Now, if you'll excuse me, I have one more patient to check on."

"Very well." Nancy eyed him for a moment longer before stepping away and allowing him to go about his business.

It was obvious she was suspicious, but he didn't owe her any explanation. They were friends, but they weren't overly close. He'd tell her eventually, along with the rest of the world. The one person he did want to tell before rumors circulated the hospital was his brother, Jason. He needed to know before the Valentine's tea party that he had promised to take Destiny to, because that was sure to get the gossip mill started.

Deciding his patient could wait a bit longer, he turned to the door leading to the staircase to head down one floor to Jason's office. He might be able to catch him there before his next surgery. The last thing he wanted was for Jason to confront him about Nora in front of others, or for the Valentine's tea party to get back to him before Brian had a chance to explain.

"I was wondering when you'd show back up to work." Jason strolled down the hallway from the opposite direction, and headed straight toward Brian.

"What?"

"I knew you were at the cabin this past weekend and you were with them." Jason opened the door to his office and nodded for Brian to follow. "I see you haven't decided yet that you need to stay away from them."

"Just the opposite." He stood with his hands in his pockets as Jason took a seat behind the desk.

"What's that supposed to mean?"

"I'm taking Destiny to the father and daughter Valentine's Day tea party here at the hospital. I thought you should know because once I do there will be nothing to keep the rumors from spreading."

Jason leaned forward, his hands clasped on top of the desk. "You've got to be joking. Have you even considered what this will do to Nora or Destiny? You're giving that little girl hope of getting a father, when there's no way you can be that for her."

"Who says I can't?"

"What?" Jason pushed forward as if he was going to stand before he thought better of it.

"Don't look at me like that. Nora is special, unlike any woman I've met before." Warmth spread through him just from thinking about her; that smile of hers lit the darkness within him. He glanced at his watch—twenty minutes until he had to be downstairs with Nora.

"If she'll allow me, I'll be there every step of the way. I'm going to be at Destiny's first treatment in just a little bit."

"What do you know about being a father?"

"What did you know about being a father until you adopted Faith?" Brian countered.

Jason shook his head. "This is different. This isn't like a new baby, you're taking on a six-year-old child."

"It's the same thing, and I'll learn. Anyway, we've taken to each other fairly well already. This isn't just about Destiny. I'm committed to Nora and they come as a package. I would hope you'd understand and be supportive. With Destiny's treatment, Nora has enough on her mind. I don't want the next gossip hitting the hospital to be that you're against what's happening with us. She doesn't need that, nor does the gossip mill."

"I'll keep my mouth shut and you can do what you want. I can't say I'm happy with this, not only because she's Jim's wife, but because of the child's condition."

"She's a widow," Brian corrected.

"The point is still the same. She married Jim. Now you think you can step into his shoes?"

"I think nothing of the kind." Brian inwardly steadied himself; it would do no good to raise his voice. Then the rumors would *really* fly. "Jim isn't here and there's no reason Nora and I can't be happy together. There's nothing to feel guilty about. If you died, would you want Liz to eventually move on and find someone who made her happy?"

"This isn't about Liz. It's about you. Damn it, Brian I want you to be happy." Jason scooted his chair back away from the desk.

"Then why can't you be happy for me?" Brian wanted to turn on his heels and go anywhere but here. They'd always been close, but this distance between them over Nora was driving him crazy.

"Is this what you really want? Wouldn't you be happy with a nice nurse, or one of Liz's friends? She could set you up again—"

Brian leaned forward, placing his hands on the desk. "No. I'm tired of the matchmaking sister-in-law. Nora is who I want, we make each other happy. Come for dinner and see us together."

"Liz said if you're happy then I should be happy for you, but I can't help but think you're getting in over your head. You already take work home with you, and you don't know how to distance yourself from the hospital. You let your patients get under your skin while you try to cure everyone."

"That makes me a good doctor," Brian reasoned.

"True, but it also stresses you out. It's not the same with me, I fix them in the operating room, and the rest of you have to deal with their daily needs." Jason shook his head. "What I'm trying to say is that taking problems home with you is one thing, but taking on a woman and her sick child is another."

"Do you even realize how heartless that sounds?" Brian straightened his back, shocked that his brother would say such a thing.

"Heartless, maybe…but I'm trying to look out for you."

"Then do us both a favor and *don't*. I love Nora and…" All of a sudden, he realized what he'd just said.

Jason leaned back in his chair and smirked. "That's what I wanted to hear you say."

"What?"

"Nora has enough going on in her life. If you aren't serious about her and Destiny, you don't deserve to be there. She doesn't need more stress, and that little girl doesn't need to be devastated in the middle of the biggest fight of her life. I fought you on this because I wanted to find out how serious you were. If you were going to leave them at the first sign of trouble, then it needed to be now."

"You did this to see if I was serious about them? Who put you in charge?" Brian couldn't believe what he was hearing. Shouldn't Jason have already known Brian better than to think he'd just disappear on Nora and Destiny?

"Liz was pissed when she found out, but Nora was the most important thing. I also wanted to remind you that no matter how hard you try, Jim will always be there. He might be dead, but he'll be a ghost in her past and there will be times she'll think about him. Are you ready for that?"

"How could she not?" Brian stepped back and lowered himself onto one of the chairs. "Jim will always be there for both of us, but I'm okay with that because I love her, and I think he would be happy about it, too. Every time I look at Destiny I can see Jim in her. She has his fighting spirit within her, and that's why I know she's going to make it through these treatments."

"What makes you think he'd approve?" Jason raised an eyebrow at him.

"He'd want Nora happy, to know that she and Destiny are taken care of. There's no reason she shouldn't love again, or that Destiny shouldn't have a father figure."

"She might not have met Jim, but she knows the man in the picture by her bedside is her father. How are you going to handle it when she asks about him? And before you ask, I peeked in on her and Nora when I first found out who she was and I saw the picture of Jim by the bed."

"I'm going to be up front. There's no reason she shouldn't know what a good man her father was, that he died to keep her safe. I won't try to be her only father, but I'll try to be there for her." He rubbed the bridge of his nose. "If it ever gets to the point that Nora and I have children of our own, there will be no differences in how they're treated. Even if things don't work out between Nora and me, I'll still be there for Destiny as long as Nora allows it. There are stories I can tell her about her father that Nora can't."

"You're okay with being second?"

"I've always been second." Brian eyed his brother.

"What's that supposed to mean?"

"You've always been first when it came to our parents. They've been more proud of your accomplishments as a doctor than they ever were with me. I might be the oldest but they hold more pride that you're a surgeon than they'll ever have with me just being a doctor." There was no disappointment in his words; it was a fact. Brian had accepted it long ago and though he was always striving to meet his goals, to accomplish things in his career, he no longer set out to please his parents, for that was one place he'd always fail. Now he lived life on his own terms, doing what made him happy and fulfilled him.

When Jason remained quiet, Brian leaned forward, placing his elbows on his knees. "I see you won't deny it."

"Mom wanted us both to follow in her father's footsteps. When you chose to become a pediatric cardiologist, she was disappointed, so there's no reason to deny it. But to say I've always been the favorite isn't true."

"Continue to live in the world of denial." Brian slapped his hands on his thighs and stood. "I won't stop you, but don't expect me to join you."

"What are you going to tell Mom?" Jason asked before Brian could open the office door.

"Nothing, at least not yet. This is my life and she wouldn't approve anyway, so I'm not even going to try." Brian took hold of the door handle. "She'll find out soon enough. I'm bringing Nora and Destiny to Faith's birthday celebration."

"Are you sure that's such a good idea?"

"Good idea or not, I'm doing it. They're a part of my life, which means they'll be in attendance for family events. Mom will have to understand that, and I don't think she'll make a fuss, not on Faith's special day with everyone there."

"Let's hope not." Jason rubbed his temples.

"If you'd prefer I not attend…"

Jason shook his head. "No, we're family. Dad will be there to keep Mom in check, so it shouldn't be too bad, though I wish you'd tell them before the party."

"If it comes up." He half-heartedly committed, and opened the door.

His mother would still be a problem later, but right now he couldn't worry about it. He needed to get downstairs to be with Nora and Destiny. That was his priority, not pleasing his parents. Those days were long gone. Thankfully.

Destiny's Wish: Cedar Grove Medical

Chapter Twelve

The treatment had gone better than Nora could have hoped for. Destiny was showing some discomfort, mostly an upset stomach coupled with exhaustion, but it had been better than the previous treatments she had gone through. Still, all Nora could do was stand by and watch. Thankfully Brian had been by her side, holding Destiny's hand as the procedure started. He'd massaged her back as they were forced to wait to see what happened, and the tension built within her. It had been more than she could have hoped for to have someone by her side.

Now she was standing in the doorway to her daughter's temporary room in Brian's house, unable to take her eyes off Destiny's sleeping form. Afraid that if she'd look away, even for a moment, things would get worse. The fear of the unknown was almost paralyzing, stealing the breath from her lungs, making her stomach roil.

"You can't stand there all night." Brian laid a hand on the small of her back.

"Just watch me."

"Nora, you know this is unreasonable. She'll call for you if she doesn't feel good."

She leaned back against him, sinking into his embrace. "I can't help but feel that if I look away even for a moment, everything will go wrong."

"That's not how this works. You've been through this before; you know the symptoms might not come right away." He pressed his lips to her temple, laying a kiss there. "She's a fighter, just like her mother."

"I think she gets that from Jim."

"That too, but don't discount yourself. You're full of fight and strength. Destiny sees that and she's not going to give up." He wrapped his arms around her waist. "You've had a long day and need to rest."

"With a week's worth of treatments, back and forth to the hospital every day, it's going to take a toll, but I can't sleep."

"You haven't tried." His hand slid over her hips. "Let's go downstairs, have a glass of wine, sit by the fire, and talk."

"Nora." Greta stood at the top of the staircase with a box in hand.

"Everything okay, Greta?" Brian asked.

Greta stepped closer, holding out the box to Nora. "I thought this might help ease your worries."

"What is it?" Nora took hold of the box but didn't open the lid.

"Baby monitor. I thought you might use it to give you peace of mind that Destiny is okay," Greta explained.

"Thank you." She lifted the lid. "No matter where I am in the house I'll be able to hear her if she needs me."

With a smile, Greta nodded. "Goodnight."

"Goodnight." Nora watched the older woman walk away before she glanced up at Brian. "You have a gem there."

"She's great. I don't know how I'd keep this house looking so well without her." He took the box from her. "Do you realize you looked away and Destiny is still resting peacefully?"

She glanced back at her daughter, still sound asleep, looking almost lost in the middle of the large bed. Nothing bad had happened when she'd looked away, but it didn't ease the worry that something was going to happen.

"I'll plug in the monitor and then we're going downstairs." He slipped past her and strolled deeper into the room while she stood frozen in place.

Instead of just standing there, she went to tuck Destiny in and feel her head for any fever. All the while telling herself she was going to be okay. Her little girl had beaten cancer before and she'd do it again. She wasn't about to let Destiny give up, and in order to help her fight, Nora had to keep her fears in check. She couldn't let the panic of the unknown paralyze her, or continue to rob her of much needed sleep. Whatever the future held was going to happen one way or another and Nora had to be at her best to help her daughter.

"Come on," Brian whispered as he switched the monitor on.

With one last glance, they strolled from the room hand in hand. It was how she hoped their future would be.

Nora snuggled against Brian's body, his warmth enveloping her, while her conscious nagged her. There was something that had woken her but she couldn't put her finger on it. She wanted to snuggle deeper beneath the covers and forget about whatever it was. A soft moan came through the monitor, and Nora shot out of bed.

"She might just be having a bad dream." Brian stretched his arms out above his head and started to get out of bed.

"You don't have to come."

"But I will." He grabbed his shirt from edge of the bed and slipped it over his head. "In case you need me."

She didn't argue, just grabbed her silk robe from the edge of the bed and shoved her arms into it. *I'm coming, Destiny.* She hurried down the hall, not bothering to tie the robe as it flapped open around her. Two doors apart and it seemed to take her longer than it had before. When she finally reached the bedroom, she found Destiny still asleep.

"See, it was a bad dream," Brian whispered as they neared the bed.

Not convinced, Nora leaned forward, brushing her hand against Destiny's forehead. "She doesn't feel warm."

"Mommy." Destiny's soft cry came as she rolled over.

"I'm here, sweetie. You were moaning, are you okay?"

"Sleepy." She answered without even opening her eyes.

"Then go back to sleep." She tucked the blankets around Destiny and pushed her hair away from her face. "I'm just down the hall if you need me. Call me and I'll hear you."

Brian stepped closer and laid a hand on her shoulder. "Come on, let's all get some sleep."

She nodded. "Don't even bother telling me you were right."

"What do you mean?" He smirked down at her before taking her hand and pulling her off the bed.

"Don't act innocent." They walked out of the bedroom before she turned back to him. "You said she'd be okay and that I was overreacting."

"Not overreacting, just worried. This study has had good results so far and Destiny has a good chance with it. There have been limited side effects, mostly what she's already experiencing."

"Limited?" Nora looked back at Destiny. "How would you like to go through the next three weeks feeling exhausted and sick to your stomach?"

"It wouldn't be the most enjoyable time, but isn't it better than the other options?" He wrapped his arm around her shoulder. "Isn't this better than going through the chemotherapy and radiation combination? I read her chart. I know how awful that was for her. We can manage these symptoms."

"Then why didn't Doctor Mathews prescribe anything?"

"We need to know how she's reacting to the treatment. This is minor, but if she's still feeling nauseous tomorrow, we'll give her something for that. The exhaustion, that isn't something we can do much about right now. You know as well as I do that it can be a standard thing for anyone fighting cancer. Their bodies are working so hard to beat the disease it leaves them exhausted."

She laid her head against his shoulder. "I just hate seeing her this way."

"I know." He laid a gentle kiss on top of her head. "Three weeks of treatment and we'll see how she does."

"But a possible six weeks is a long time if it hasn't killed all the cancer cells." She wanted her happy, healthy, little girl back. The one who couldn't get enough time in the pool and loved helping Greta bake cookies at the cabin. Her little girl was missing out on her childhood.

"The treatments will be over before you know it."

"Then what do I do?" She turned to face him. "Just when I thought we had put the cancer behind us, it's suddenly back with a vengeance. How do I know it won't do the same thing in a few years?"

"We don't know, but you can't live your life in fear. She fought it once and she'll do it again. We'll both be at her side to make sure she gets through this."

It had taken her nearly three years to get the constant fear out of her mind. To not become terrified every time Destiny had a cold. All of a sudden those fears were back and she couldn't push them away. Cancer was a part of their life again. This time she wasn't sure she could just forget about it no matter the outcome.

Maybe forgetting about it was the wrong idea. Instead, maybe she needed to do something to make a positive impact. To take a bad thing and turn it around into something constructive. *Hope's Toy Chest.*

Chapter Thirteen

The week had flown by. As surprising as it was to Nora, Destiny's condition didn't worsen with the daily treatments. She was still exhausted, but at least the nausea had settled down with the medication Doctor Mathews prescribed, only rearing its ugly head shortly after each treatment. It gave her hope that they'd be able to get through this, even if it went on for the full six weeks.

It was Friday, the last day of treatments for the week. Nora slipped out to the coffee pot in the hall, to pour herself another refill, when she spotted Chelsea Mathews coming out of her husband's office. Without thinking twice, she held up a new cup. "Would you like to join me?"

"No coffee for me, thanks. I've had to cut it out since I'm pregnant, and I doubt there's any tea."

"Actually there's one tea bag left—apple cinnamon." Nora plucked the last tea package out of the basket.

"Well, in that case, sure."

"I wanted to talk to you about Hope's Toy Chest." She tore open the tea bag package, placed it in the cup, and added hot water. "Have you hired someone for the position yet?"

"No, I interviewed a few candidates this week but none of them seemed perfect. Kingsley thinks I'm just being picky and don't actually want to hire someone." Chelsea added two packages of sugar to the tea and stirred. "Why, do you know someone who might be interested in the position?"

"Actually, I'd like to apply. I typed up a resume and had planned to give it to Doctor Mathews to give to you after today's treatment." Nora took her coffee and stepped away from the counter, moving away from the nurse's station to give them a little privacy. "I'm not sure I'm what you have in mind for this position, and I understand either way. However, I'd love to find some way of helping the organization."

"I don't need a resume if you have a few minutes to talk. Go over what experiences you have. We can discuss Hope's Toy Chest and go from there."

"Destiny's sleeping while the IV finishes, so I have some time."

Chelsea nodded toward the door she'd exited a few minutes before. "If Kingsley is done with his call, let's use his office. You'll be close and we don't have to stand in the hallway discussing this." She opened the door and then pushed it wider. "Mind if we come in?"

"Sure." He nodded to the chairs in front of his desk. "Everything okay?"

"Nora has shown interest in the position and I wanted to speak with her about Hope's Toy Chest," Chelsea explained as they entered, and she shut the door behind them.

"Well then, I'll do my rounds and leave you two alone." He came around the desk, leaned down to Chelsea, and gave her a quick kiss. "I'll keep my fingers crossed that Nora's the one."

"You just want me to hire someone so you know things will be fine for the first holiday season with the baby, and I won't be stressing over every little detail." Chelsea shook her head at her husband.

"That, and because Nora understands why Hope's Toy Chest is special. That means more to you than someone with all the perfect qualifications, or you'd have hired that other woman. This isn't just some organization you've thrown together, it's your heart and soul. You wouldn't just trust anyone with it." Without another word, he opened the door and left.

"He's right." Chelsea set the tea aside. "Hope's Toy Chest is more than just an organization I threw together because I needed something to do with my time."

"That's obvious, not just from what I've heard but from the paperwork in our check-out folder. It's not just about bringing toys to the sick children, though that's a big part of it. You've also put together a support system for the parents, activities for the children, and so much more."

"I see you've done your research." Chelsea smirked.

"I have. At first, I just wanted to know more about it, but over the last few days I've realized I want to be a part of it."

"Why just the last few days?"

Nora took a seat and wiped her hands on her jeans. "When you came to the house, I said I would be interested in getting involved. At that time I thought I could help by wrapping some gifts, chatting with families, or something like that. It was Brian who suggested I put my name in for the position. But I held off because of Destiny's cancer. I wanted to make sure I could do the job without the distractions."

"Why the change? Have you decided you can do it?"

"Yes, I guess I have. Destiny is taking well to the treatments. Doctor Mathews believes it's working, the blood test results are coming back as he'd like them. All I can do is be there for her, but I need more purpose. I need something for me, to give back and to keep me busy."

Chelsea took the other chair in front of her husband's desk. "We're getting ahead of ourselves. Let's backtrack for a moment. Do you have any charity or work experience?"

"Until Destiny was born, I was involved in charity work, mostly visiting injured military personnel at the hospital, talking with their families, making sure their needs were met, and sending care packages to overseas service members. See, my husband was in the Army and this was my way of making the most out of military life, and it was a way to ease the loneliness. When he was killed in action, that ended. I was pregnant with Destiny and…well, honestly, I fell apart. When she was born, I was able to get myself together again." Nora looked down at her hands as she thought of those months of loneliness; it had hurt so bad she wasn't sure she'd make it through.

"Work experience?" Chelsea pushed when Nora remained silent.

"Until I moved to Montana to bring Destiny to Cedar Grove Children's Hospital, I had been employed as a virtual assistant for a marketing firm, mostly writing press releases, following up on details for events, little things like that. It allowed me to be home with Destiny. I was there for a little over three years."

"If it was virtual, why did it end?"

"My boss needed someone to attend an upcoming event and I couldn't, not with Destiny's health. My daughter had to come first, even though I did love my job."

"I'm sorry things ended like that, but you know Brian and Kingsley might just be right. You might be perfect for this position. Your marketing experience is an advantage. I'm always wanting to take Hope's Toy Chest to the next level. I think you could help with that."

"I'll do whatever I can. Like your husband said, this charity means something to me and that's what's important. If given the chance, I can prove to you that I can manage Destiny's care and this position without letting either of them slack."

"I have no doubt." Chelsea nodded. "You're hired."

Over the next hour, they discussed everything the job would entail. Covering the different events that were already scheduled, but most importantly going over the big Christmas push. Even though it was just days before Valentine's Day, they needed to think ahead, especially with Chelsea due in September.

While Destiny received her treatments, Chelsea and Nora would meet in Kingsley's office to go over the details of Hope's Toy Chest.

Where each event stood and what still needed to be done. They'd work together until Chelsea was sure Nora could handle things on her own. Even once the baby was born, Chelsea still planned to be active within the organization. They'd work together, a team for the cause.

Nora still couldn't believe she'd gotten the position, and her ideas for the organization jumbled in her thoughts. This was a new beginning for her. A way to make this horrible situation better, not only for her but for the other families. Hope's Toy Chest was giving Nora her hope back.

Seeing Brian's car pull into the drive, Nora left Destiny lying in bed watching her favorite movie on the television he had given her days before. They had decided this was easier than making her comfortable on the sofa and hauling her back upstairs to bed once she was too tired to walk or had fallen asleep in the middle of a movie. She headed down the steps in a light jog, eager to tell him the news.

"Ms. Horton, is everything okay?" Greta stopped dusting to look her way.

"Yes, fine, thanks." She shot Greta a big smile. "I just need to talk to Brian."

"Whatever it's about, you look happy about it." Greta grabbed a rag off the end table. "I'll give you some privacy and get dinner started."

"Thank you." Nora reached out to take hold of the handle just as the door flung open, forcing her to take a step back out of surprise. "Oh."

"What's wrong?" Brian asked, slipping off his coat. "Is Destiny okay?"

"Everything's fine, no…it's wonderful. I got the position with Hope's Toy Chest," she blurted out, not waiting until he had a chance to hang up his coat.

"That's wonderful. I'm so happy for you." He wrapped his arms around her and lifted her off the ground. "I know you're going to be amazing. We should celebrate."

"Not tonight." She kept her arms around his neck as he lowered her to her feet. "Greta has dinner started and Destiny is exhausted. I haven't told her either, I wanted you to be the first one to know."

"Then tomorrow. Destiny and I have a date for the hospital's tea party, then tomorrow night is Faith's birthday party. How about the next day, the two of us will go out for a quiet meal. Greta can watch over Destiny while we're gone." He rubbed his thumb along her jawline. "Say yes."

"Okay. Unless we get a call approving us for the rental."

"What rental?" His body went rigid under her touch.

"After Destiny's treatment, I had an appointment to see an apartment. It's a little farther from the hospital than I would like, but it seems like a decent neighborhood. There's a playground across the street where Destiny can play outside when she's feeling better."

"I didn't know you were looking." He stepped back from their embrace, the sadness creasing around his mouth.

"You knew things couldn't stay the way they are. You don't need Destiny and I hanging around here." As much as she hated to leave, she couldn't outstay her welcome. He had invited her there so Destiny could get out of the hospital.

He reached out and took her hand. "I want you and Destiny to stay. I want you in my life, in my home, and in my bed. Nora, I love you."

Love. He loved her.

She wasn't sure what to say to that, or how to handle it. She should have seen this coming, especially after they had been sleeping together since that night in the cabin, but she hadn't, and it shook her world.

Chapter Fourteen

The hour was late, but Nora sat on the sofa with a book in hand, her eyes fluttering shut. She was determined to wait up until she could talk to Brian. When he'd admitted his love for her, she wasn't sure what to say, and was relieved when Destiny called for her. When she had be able to get her thoughts together and get Destiny asleep, she came downstairs to find he'd been called back to the hospital for an emergency. Now, as the minutes ticked by, she waited for him to return. With each passing second, her nervousness grew.

She thought she knew what she was going to say to him but as the hours rushed past she respectively questioned her plan. Whatever came out of her mouth when he walked in might very well surprise them both. One thing was for sure, she needed to say something to ease the mounting tension left between them. There was so much of it he didn't even bother to tell her he had to go back to the hospital; instead he'd scrawled a note for her that she'd found in his office when she went to look for him.

Unable to keep her eyes open any longer, she set the book aside and scooted down on the sofa until she could rest her head against the armrest. She'd sleep there until he came home, with the light on so he'd see her when he came in. She didn't feel right going to bed in his room without him, especially after the way they had left things earlier, and sleeping in the guest room would give the wrong impression.

Invisible weights pulled her eyelids shut and sleep called to her like a distant friend. Her body begged her to give in, to sleep for a little bit before the dawn of a new day. The only thing that stopped her was the sound of the front door opening. *Brian.*

"It's late. You didn't have to wait up for me." He stood in the doorway, his face drawn with worry.

"Is everything okay?" She pushed herself up into the sitting position.

"Only time will tell."

"Are you talking about something at the hospital or about us?"

"Both." He untied his tie, sliding the silky material free from the collar of his dress shirt. "Look, Nora, I'm sorry for earlier."

"Sorry for what you said…or how you said it?" She tried to swallow past the lump that had formed in her throat, but the fear of his next words made that nearly impossible.

"I shouldn't have said it like I did."

"So, you *do* love me?" She needed to hear it again to know it was true.

He nodded. "I should have eased into it, instead I blurted it out, catching you off guard. You've got a lot on your mind right now and I realize you need time, but I want you to know that I'm here for you, even if you don't return my feelings."

She rose from the sofa, stretching out her muscles from curling up in one position for so long. "I do." Her voice broke and she took a deep breath before regaining control. "After Jim died I was sure I'd never love someone again, but then you came into my life. You've proven to me that I can love someone without dishonoring Jim's memory. He'll always be a part of my past, but I can still have a future. A future with you."

"Nora…"

She came to stand in front of him, placing her finger in front of his lips, cutting him off. "I'm saying that I love you, and I hope you can accept that no matter my feelings for you, my love for Jim will always be there, too. Destiny is his daughter and there will come a time she'll want to know more about him. If you're okay with that, I think we can build on what we have here."

"I'm not trying to take Jim's place in your heart, or in Destiny's. I just want to be with you, in whatever way you can accept. I love you, Nora, and I love Destiny." He wrapped his arms around her waist. "I want you in my life and here. Don't move out."

"I can't stay here forever."

"Why not?" He raised his eyebrow in question.

"What will everyone think? It was one thing to come here temporarily while I searched for a place."

"Then throw caution to the wind and marry me."

"What?" She leaned back, nearly breaking his hold around her waist.

"You heard me, marry me." He gave a light, heartfelt laugh that caressed over her skin. "There I go blurting things out again, but I've never been happier than I am now with you and Destiny in my life."

The wall clock struck two in the morning and she smirked. "A Valentine's Day proposal. How can a girl say no?"

"Is that a yes?"

She nodded. "Yes. I'd be honored to be Mrs. West." He leaned in close, claiming her mouth as if sealing the deal.

Here's to new beginnings.

The father-daughter tea party went off without a hitch and Brian's time with Destiny had an ease to it. They had meshed together, and even without Nora there to accompany them, they had gotten along fine. Now, on the ride home, she seemed in a better mood than she had been since the treatments had begun.

"Mommy said she's marrying you. Will that make you my husband, too?"

A smile pulled at the corners of his lips. Husband? That was too sweet, and reminded him that kids had a way of saying the cutest things. Sometimes it was more embarrassing, and other instances were just so innocent as this had been. He glanced in the rearview mirror at his soon-to-be daughter. The way her brown hair was pulled back from her face in a braid, and the pink and white dress, made her look like any other six-year-old girl.

Thankfully he had already discussed with Nora how they'd handle things with Destiny. They had planned to file the adoption paperwork so she'd legally be his daughter as well, and have her name changed to West. That had been Nora's idea to make them a complete family, so if they had children of their own there would be no differences in their names. They were going to be open with her, letting her know he'd be her father. She'd be lucky and have two daddies, one there in person and the other with angel wings.

"No, I'll be your mom's husband and your dad."

"My wish." She leaned forward. "I'll have a real daddy like other girls."

He nodded. "You'll always have a date for the father-daughter tea parties."

She bounced in her seat. "Does that mean I can call you Daddy?"

"If you want." That wasn't something they had thought about in the early morning hours when they were going over Destiny's possible questions, but if he was going to raise her as his own daughter it only seemed right she'd call him Daddy.

"I finally got a Daddy. It's the best present in the world." He pulled into the driveway, put the car in park, and she unhooked her seatbelt. "I've got to tell Mommy." She opened the door and skipped toward the house before he had managed to get his own door open. It was nice to see her energy back, even if it was only for a little while. He got out of the car and followed after her, just as Nora opened the front door.

"Mommy!" Destiny sped her pace. "Guess what?"

"What, sweetie? Did you have a good time?" She knelt before her daughter.

"Yeah, but it got better on the car ride home. Did you know he's going to be my daddy? My wish came true."

"I did know that." She nodded to her daughter, while her gaze found his.

"I've got to tell Greta." Destiny rushed past Nora, straight into the house.

"Well, she's certainly excited." Nora stood back up.

"At least I got her corrected before she came running to you to tell you that I was going to be her husband." He let out a deep laugh and laced his arm around her.

"What?"

"On the car ride home she wanted to know if I would be her husband, too, since I'm marrying you." They stepped inside, and he shut the door behind them before he turned back to her, wrapping his arms around her waist. "It was so cute."

"Kids say the damnedest things."

"That they do. So, when are we going to make it official? I want you as my wife as soon as possible."

"I was thinking about this while you were gone." She took his hand and led them toward the living room. "I just want something small. You friends from the hospital, Chelsea and Kingsley, and your family, so I was thinking maybe we could do it here. If we wait until summer we can do it outside in the garden."

"Or we can do it sooner, inside. There's enough room for the people who matter."

"That works, I just wasn't sure if you wanted everyone inside or not."

He sat down on the sofa and drew her down to sit on his lap. "I host a Christmas party each year, this wouldn't be any different. How about the last Saturday in March? That will give you six weeks to plan it."

"Give me four weeks. One month from today."

He leaned closer, his face hovering next to hers. "I can't wait." He pressed his lips to hers, his tongue sliding into her mouth, and she returned his kisses with the same eagerness until the doorbell rang. He pulled back and sighed. "Why do I think whoever's at that door isn't bringing good news?"

"Could it be about Destiny? Or one of your patients at the hospital?"

He shook his head. "I have a feeling it's even worse than that. My parents."

Destiny's Wish: Cedar Grove Medical

Chapter Fifteen

Just as Brian had suspected, he opened the door to find his mother standing there. The morning had gone so perfectly, and now this was happening before he could even prepare Nora for what to expect. His good mood soured. His father wasn't around, which only made it worse. Dad was always good at keeping Mom in check.

"It's cold out here, aren't you going to invite me in?" his mother snapped.

He stepped back, letting her pass. "What are you doing here? I thought we were meeting at Jason's tonight for Faith's birthday party."

"We were, until I spoke to Liz and she let me know that you're bringing someone." His mother eyed him. "It seemed to be some big secret because when she realized I didn't know both Liz and Jason refused to speak any further on the subject. Who is this woman?"

"My name's Nora Horton," she announced as she came up behind his mother.

Lillian spun on her heels to face Nora. "Horton...*Jim* Horton?" The women eyed each other for a long moment. "You're his wife. What are you doing here?"

He stepped around his mother to stand by Nora's side. He slipped his arm around her shoulders, tired of explaining she wasn't his wife. "Widow, and she's my fiancée now."

"Your what?" Lillian stepped forward.

"Mommy, Mommy." Destiny came running toward Nora. "Greta said we could make cookies. Can I please?"

"Sure, sweetie, but why don't you change first? I don't want you to get anything on your pretty dress. That way, you can wear it tonight to the party." She tucked a stray hair behind Destiny's ear.

"Mommy, who is the lady?"

"She's my mother," Brian explained. "Now run along and change so you can make one of those cookies especially for me."

"Okay, Daddy." She skipped from the room toward the staircase.

"Daddy?" Lillian spat the word as if it was poison.

"I told you Nora and I are to be married. We've set a wedding date for one month from today. That will make Destiny my daughter." He tipped his head toward the living room. "Why don't we have a seat?"

"Nora, I think you should excuse us. I need to speak with my son *alone*."

"Mom, there's nothing you can say or do that will change this. Nora and I are getting married, so be supportive or not...that's your choice." He kept his arm around Nora and went to the sofa. "Where's Dad?"

"He's at the hotel room. After finding out there was an unknown woman moving in on his son, he became ill."

He highly doubted that, but his mother always had a way of turning things around to make him feel bad. It was more likely that his father had been ill because he refused to listen to his doctors. He wouldn't cut out the spicy foods, so his ulcer always flared up until he was miserable.

"I hope he'll be well enough to attend Faith's party tonight."

"That's the second thing I came over here about." Lillian took a seat across from the sofa. "Jason has an emergency surgery so they've postponed the party."

"If this is because you found out about my engagement and threw a fit—"

"No, you can check. Jason's performing surgery tonight, a heart transplant. He was leaving for the hospital when I came over. Though, you're right about one thing…I'm not happy about *this*." She waved her hands at them. "You haven't seen each other in years and suddenly you're getting married."

"These last few weeks with her have been the happiest of my life." He placed his hand on Nora's leg. "I know the woman she is and I love her. That should be enough for you."

"Mrs. West, I realized this happened quickly."

"Damn right it did." Lillian eyed Nora. "How do I know you're not just after his money?"

"How dare you?" Nora scooted forward as if she was going to take off, but he held her there.

"Mom, I will not stand for you coming in here and insulting her."

"His finances have nothing to do with the love I have for him," Nora snapped. "Jim and the military made sure I would be able to provide for myself and Destiny. I'll sign a pre-nuptial agreement if that will make you happy, but please don't come here and accuse me of something you know nothing about."

He took hold of her hand, proud that she'd stood up to his mother. He needed someone with a backbone, someone who wouldn't let his mother try to control things. "A pre-nuptial agreement is out of the question," he said firmly.

"Are you out of your mind, Brian?" Lillian hummed. "Make her sign one."

"No, it's about trust and love. Mother, this has nothing to do with you."

"If she's not after your money, then why is she living here? She's been here for a while." Lillian smirked at them as if she'd thought of the perfect argument.

"This is my home and I asked them here. There's no reason for them to move when we'll be married in a month's time." He rubbed his thumb along the contours of Nora's hand, trying to ease the tension he could see building within her. "I want you to respect my fiancée, our relationship, and our decisions, without trying to add your stance on it."

"You are my son. I have a say when you're making a disastrous mistake."

"That's where you're wrong." Still keeping his hand in Nora's, he leaned forward. "You've never approved of my life or the career path—"

"You would have made an excellent surgeon."

"See what I mean." He let go of Nora and stood. "I went into medicine just like you always wanted. That should have been good enough, but it never was. Jason enjoys his specialty, but he has to deal with more stress. It's noticeable in the way he carries himself, how he deals with his family, and in every aspect of his life. I never wanted that. I thought you'd be happy enough that I became a doctor, but it was never enough for you."

"You could have been better, done more."

"You've always pushed for more and more." His heart pounded, his stomach churned. He wanted to scream at her, but he wouldn't. Not in front of Nora. "I'm happy with my career. I make a difference in my patients' lives. I'm happy with Nora and Destiny. It's time you accept this is my life and stop pushing. I'm not like Jason, I won't keep working my ass off to make you happy. I learned a long time ago it was never going to happen." He shoved his hands into his pockets in agitation, his body rigid. "Jason became a surgeon to make you happy. He's a damn good one, maybe even the best at Cedar Grove Children's Hospital. Now you're pushing for him to make head of surgery when the position comes available at the end of the year. When he does that, you'll start pushing for the next goal you have in mind for him."

"What's wrong with having goals for your children?"

"There's a time when enough is enough. You can't keep pushing and pushing. I'll never give you that kind of control over my life. What I do is to make *me* happy."

"You proved your independence when you chose to become a pediatric cardiologist." Lillian spat out the words as if they caused a bad taste in her mouth.

"Obviously not enough." He stood next to the fireplace, placing his hand on the mantle. "Mom, we're family and I love you. I've accepted that my decisions will never make you happy and I'm fine with it. Now I ask you to accept that Nora and Destiny are going to be a part of this family, and for you to welcome them with open arms. None of us need the extra tension, and you should welcome another grandchild."

"Not a biological one."

"If Brian can accept my daughter as his, why can't you?" Nora shot up from the sofa, her face red with fury.

"Darling." Brian let go of the mantle and stepped closer.

"No, I've been sitting here quietly and listening as she puts down your career and even me, but I won't have her making Destiny think she is less important just because she wasn't born into this family." Nora turned back to Lillian. "Faith was adopted and she's not biologically either Jason's or Liz's, but from the way your eyes lit up when you spoke about her, I don't think you care."

"That's a different situation."

Brian came to stand next to Nora. "Why? Because Liz couldn't produce a grandchild for you, due to the cancer treatments she had as a child? Or because Jason has always been your pride and joy?"

"When Jason chose to marry her, we knew they'd never be able to have children of their own. You, on the other hand…I had hoped you would at the very least give me one grandchild to carry on our bloodline."

"Just because I have a daughter doesn't mean we won't have other children." Nora slipped her hand into Brian's.

"I'm filing the paperwork to officially adopt Destiny so that if and when we have other children they will all have the same last name. There will be no differences in how the children are treated by *anyone*." Brian stressed those words, hoping his mother would get the idea.

"Seems like you have it all figured out." Lillian rose from the chair and ran her hands down the front of her dress. "I wish you all the best. Taking on a child of that age, a child who is clearly sick, will not be an easy task. Your marriage will have a battle before it even gets started."

"One we'll fight together and win. Destiny's a special little girl." Brian eyed his mother, not sure if he had won this argument or if she she'd just given up.

"How did you know she was sick?" Nora questioned.

"It's clear from her body size and the way she carries herself. I wouldn't be surprised if it was a heart issue which led you to finding Brian after all this time."

"Actually, it's cancer," Nora explained. "She's going through treatment and will be fine."

Lillian just nodded and strolled from the room. Instead of seeing his mother out, he listened until they heard the front door opening and shutting. He turned to Nora and wrapped his arms around her waist. "I'm sorry about my mother."

"That's not your fault. Parents sometimes never seem able to let go." She laid her head against his chest. "Your mother doesn't seem supportive of this."

"No surprise there, she's never been supportive of my choices, but that doesn't matter. Just hang in there and I promise she'll come around."

"Don't worry, she doesn't scare me. I just feel bad that she's against us, and I'm serious if you want me to sign a pre-nup—"

He tangled his fingers in her hair, using his gentle grip to tilt her head back just enough so she would look up at him. "Stop, I'll hear nothing of it. I love you, and I know if you were marrying me for anything else it wouldn't be for my money but to have an in-house doctor." His lips curled into a smile.

"Your doctor skills come in handy." She replied to his tease with one of her own. "So, yeah, I think that's a good reason to marry you. Plus, I think I could find a few more uses for you."

"I feel so cheap." His chuckle was light, laced with a hum of amusement.

Nora was the best thing that had ever happened to him. Where once only darkness and work resided in his life, Nora had brought laughter and joy. He had never been happier than he was with her by his side. Love made him a different person, a happier one.

Epilogue

The world seemed to stop spinning as Nora sat there in the living room, holding Destiny's latest test results. After six weeks of treatments, her cancer was nearly gone—but nearly wasn't enough. They needed it to be completely in remission.

"What now?" She glanced up at Kingsley who was sitting across from her.

"Destiny's results show the treatment is working, and besides her fatigue there have been few side effects."

"She still has cancer." She swallowed past the lump in her throat and blinked away the tears that were threatening to fall. "What is our next course of action?"

"I'd like to give her a week-long break and then begin the treatments again. Another six weeks should kill all the remaining cancer cells."

"The studies that have already been conducted have been for a max of six weeks." Brian grabbed the paper and read it over before taking hold of Nora's hand. "What additional consequences could there be for doubling the treatment?"

"We don't know." Kingsley shook his head. "Destiny will be the first to go past the six weeks recommended, but I feel this is her best chance. It's either continue this treatment or do the chemotherapy and radiation, which is what we've been trying to avoid."

"You want to experiment more on my daughter." Dark spots danced within her vision.

"No, I want to make her healthy again." He scooted to the edge of the chair and took her other hand. "You can see these treatments have worked. Look at how much the tumor has shrunk, the blood results show dramatic changes. This is her best chance."

"I don't know." She had counted down the days until the treatments would be over, praying her little girl would be in remission again. Now the world dropped out from under her.

"I'll monitor her condition carefully and we'll take each treatment one step at a time to see how she reacts to it. You've come this far to stay away from the other options, we can't give up now."

"Brian?" She glanced at him.

"I think we have no other option. She's nearly there. We know what the other choice is and how badly she reacted to the radiation. I know you don't want to put her through that again." He squeezed her hand. "This is Kingsley's specialty, if he believes it's the best course of action for us, then I trust him. We don't know what happens with additional treatments because it hasn't been done yet, but we'll all be there for her. She'll get through this."

"Okay." She nodded. "One treatment at a time and we'll see how it goes. If she gets sick from this, we'll reconsider our options."

"I apologize for interrupting, Nora." Greta stood in the doorway to the living room, the portable phone in her hand. "It's the call you've been waiting for."

"Please excuse me, this is important. Kingsley, don't leave, I'll be right back." Nora rose from the sofa, her heart fluttering in her chest. She hoped this would be the call that proved she was capable of doing what Chelsea needed for Hope's Toy Chest.

Taking the phone from Greta, Nora stepped out of the living room and moved down the hallway. "Hello."

"Mrs. West."

Nora paused for a moment before answering, still trying to get used to being Mrs. West. "Yes, this is she."

"I'm Trina Winston, Leena's assistant, and I'm returning your call about the possibility of her doing a benefit concert. She's on tour until June and is due back in the studio in September. Did you have a date in mind for this benefit?"

"I realize her schedule is hectic, so I'm willing to work with any time frame she can provide. It would be an honor to have her come perform."

"One moment, please." There was a shuffling noise, and then Trina said something to someone else before another voice came on the line.

"Nora, this is Leena. I remember you, though you were Nora Horton then. I was told you were no longer with my promotional company."

"That's correct. My daughter was diagnosed with cancer and I moved to Montana so she could go through treatments. It gave me an opportunity to reconnect with an old friend who's a doctor at the hospital, and one thing led to another." Nora leaned against the wall. "When the idea of us doing a benefit concert came up, I immediately thought of you."

"Because of my sister," Leena supplied.

"I'm sorry, but yes. I thought because of your past experience with this disease, you might be interested in helping us raise money to benefit the lives of these children."

"That's why I'm doing it." Leena paused for a moment. "Any day in July and I'll be there. Once you've set up the venue, you can contact me directly at—"

"One moment, let me grab a pen."

"Don't worry about it. I have your cell phone number, I'll text you my information."

"Thank you."

"No, thank *you*." Leena let out a deep sigh. "This couldn't have come at a better time for me."

The call ended and Nora couldn't believe her luck. "Holy crap!" She set the phone on the hall table. This connection had been made when she'd been with the marketing firm, and now it was giving her the biggest break possible for Hope's Toy Chest.

"The news you were waiting for?"

She looked down the hall to find Brian standing there with Kingsley by his side. "Yes." The smile stretching over her face couldn't be etched off with a chisel. "Kingsley, could you pass on a message to Chelsea?"

"Sure, I'm heading to meet her for dinner right now. She texted me that she was craving hot wings, so we're going to the chicken place in town."

"Tell her I got Leena for the benefit concert. I'll call tomorrow to book the venue."

"Leena, the country singer?" He sounded surprised as he took his coat from Brian.

"That's her. She'll do a benefit concert for Hope's Toy Chest in July."

"Wow, you really are the perfect fit for this. I know Chelsea is glad to have the help." He buttoned his coat. "I've got to go, can't keep the wife waiting. Just remember not to stress about Destiny and the additional treatments. Your little girl is strong, she's going to make it through this, and we'll be watching her."

"Thanks." Brian opened the door for Kingsley. "I appreciate you coming here to tell us."

With the door closed, Brian turned to her. "You okay?"

"I'm worried about Destiny, and extending her treatments, but he's right. We're going to get through this. With you by my side, I know everything's going to be okay." She crossed the distance between them.

"I'm so proud of you." He wrapped his arms around her waist and drew her against him. "All the work you've done to get Leena and this benefit concert is going to pay off. When do we get to tell Destiny that Leena's coming here?"

"Not until I get the contracts signed. I don't want her spreading it around the hospital until it's official." She laced her arms around his neck. "Instead of telling me how proud you are of my work, why don't we go upstairs and you can make me forget about these upcoming treatments?"

"That could be arranged." He lifted her into his arms and strolled toward the staircase.

"I still can't believe we're married. Two weeks later, and I still can't get used to someone calling me Mrs. West."

"Believe it, because in another week, Destiny will be a West as well."

She had the family she thought she'd lost when Jim died. Love had finally been brought back into her life, and she couldn't have been happier.

Marissa Dobson

Born and raised in the Pittsburgh, Pennsylvania area, Marissa Dobson now resides about an hour from Washington, D.C. She's a lady who likes to keep busy, and is always busy doing something. With two different college degrees, she believes you're never done learning.

Being the first daughter to an avid reader, this gave her the advantage of learning to read at a young age. Since learning to read she has always had her nose in a book. It wasn't until she was a teenager that she started writing down the stories she came up with.

Marissa is blessed with a wonderful supportive husband, Thomas. He's her other half and allows her to stay home and pursue her writing. He puts up with all her quirks and listens to her brainstorm in the middle of the night.

Her writing buddies Max (a cocker spaniel) and Dawne (a beagle mix) are always around to listen to her bounce ideas off them. They might not be able to answer, but they are helpful in their own ways.

She love to hear from readers so send her an email at marissa@marissadobson.com or visit her online at http://www.marissadobson.com.

Destiny's Wish: Cedar Grove Medical

Other Books by Marissa Dobson

Alaskan Tigers:
Tiger Time
The Tiger's Heart
Tigress for Two
Night with a Tiger
Trusting a Tiger
Jinx's Mate
Two for Protection
Bearing Secrets

Stormkin:
Storm Queen

Reaper:
A Touch of Death

Beyond Monogamy:

Theirs to Tresure

SEALed for You:

Ace in the Hole

Explosive Passion

Capturing a Diamond

Operation Family

Cedar Grove Medical:

Hope's Toy Chest

Destiny's Wish

Fate Series:

Snowy Fate

Sarah's Fate

Mason's Fate

As Fate Would Have It

Half Moon Harbor Resort:

Learning to Live

Learning What Love Is

Her Cowboy's Heart

Half Moon Harbor Resort Volume One

Clearwater:

Winterbloom

Unexpected Forever

Losing to Win

Christmas Countdown

The Surrogate

Clearwater Romance Volume One

Small Town Doctor

Stand Alone:

Starting Over

Secret Valentine

Restoring Love

The Twelve Seductive Days of Christmas

CPSIA information can be obtained at www.ICGtesting.com
Printed in the USA
LVOW07s1630100515

437948LV00001B/159/P